10/23
6/20
B

THE HAUNTING OF HENRY DAVIS

ALSO BY KATHRYN SIEBEL

The Trouble with Twins

THE HAUNTING OF HENRY DAVIS

KATHRYN SIEBEL

Alfred A. Knopf
New York

For Gerry
with love

Text copyright © 2019 by Kathryn Siebel
Jacket art and interior illustrations copyright © 2019 by Celia Krampien

All rights reserved. Published in the United States by Alfred A. Knopf, an imprint of Random House Children's Books, a division of Penguin Random House LLC, New York.

Knopf, Borzoi Books, and the colophon are registered trademarks of Penguin Random House LLC.

Visit us on the Web! rhcbooks.com

Educators and librarians, for a variety of teaching tools, visit us at RHTeachersLibrarians.com

Library of Congress Cataloging-in-Publication Data is available upon request.
ISBN 978-1-101-93277-3 (trade) — ISBN 978-1-101-93278-0 (lib. bdg.) — ISBN 978-1-101-93279-7 (ebook)

Printed in the United States of America
July 2019
10 9 8 7 6 5 4 3 2 1

First Edition

Random House Children's Books supports the First Amendment and celebrates the right to read.

We chase after ghosts and spirits
and are left holding only memories
and dreams.

CHARLES DE LINT,
Moonlight and Vines

CHAPTER ONE

THE NEW KID

If you want my actual opinion, I'd have to say that it comes down to this: either you believe in them or you don't. Ghosts, I mean. Sometimes that changes suddenly, of course. Usually, when one shows up in the middle of the night. But let's just say you're a skeptic, a doubter, like I was. I can respect that. Then, you have to start where I always do—with some research. And you have to be ready to uncover some things that you honestly can't explain. So let me just tell you this one story. It's about a woman in England who claimed her daughter was reincarnated and started to remember every bit of her past life.

It seems they were driving in the country one day, and the little girl made her mother stop the car in front of this random house. She *screamed* at her mother until she did it. And then she hopped right out and pushed through the gate and ran toward this cottage—in the middle of nowhere. Her mother followed her, of course.

"What is it?" the mother asked.

"I think I used to live here," the girl said. "I'm sure I did."

Creepy, right? And how would you have liked to be inside, sipping your tea or whatever, when the two of them showed up?

And then there are the kids with the "invisible friends." Pretty common, really. Nobody else can see them except the kid. But they're all alone in their room just chattering away. What explains that?

Or sometimes it's an animal, maybe a dog. And it just stops in its tracks at a certain spot and starts barking like crazy. At nothing?

But maybe it's something less obvious, the way it was for me—with Henry. I don't know how to explain it except to say that from the minute he walked into Ms. Biniam's class on the first day of the fifth grade, there was something, well, *familiar* about Henry—which was impossible, really, because I'd never seen him before in my life. I guess you could call it déjà vu. You know, the feeling that you already recognize a place, or a person, from the first moment. It's a real thing, and nobody understands exactly how it works—except some scientists say it's your brain confusing the past and the present. Or maybe, like with that little girl in England, it's one lifetime overlapping the next. I don't pretend I can explain it all, even after everything that happened with Henry.

All I know is that Henry appeared that first day of school in the doorway of our classroom. And he was late. Biniam was already taking attendance and telling us where to sit.

"Henry Davis," Ms. Biniam said, looking around.

"Here," said Henry.

He took a step toward her, no doubt trying to ignore the fact that every kid in the room was staring at him. Even aside from being late, Henry didn't make a great first impression. It almost seemed like he was trying hard not to. First off, there was the way he dressed. He could have made *Guinness World Records* for Biggest Nerd looking like that. His pants were much too short, his glasses were strapped onto his head with one of those elastic straps that should never leave the basketball court, and his T-shirt said *Karsoff Chess Academy—Your Move!*

The rest of us were waiting in our pods—the little squares of desks that Ms. Biniam had assigned us. Across from me was Zack Martin, the biggest kid in class. He had a buzz cut, braces, and a fairly bad attitude. Kitty-corner was Renee Garcia, who had the longest hair and the darkest brown eyes I'd ever seen. Then, next to me, was an empty desk that I knew, somehow, belonged to Henry Davis.

When Biniam sent Henry our way, Zack made a little grunting sound and said, "Figures." Then he slumped even farther down in his seat and stuck one big foot out toward Henry, so that Henry tripped and crash-landed into the seat next to me. That's how fifth grade started for Henry. Biniam gave Zack the first of about a thousand glares she would aim his way before the year was up.

And Henry, well, poor Henry. He looked pale and exhausted. How else was he supposed to look? I didn't know it yet, of course, but that morning Henry Davis had seen his very first ghost.

I couldn't do anything about Ms. Biniam's seating chart, but outside class, I didn't spend much time with Henry at the beginning. My mother, like every mother since the dawn of time, always reminded me to be nice to the new kid. And it wasn't that I was mean to Henry. I said hello to him when he sat down next to me each morning. I was friendly. But I didn't exactly go out of my way to spend time with him. And that's just how it is, mostly, with new kids. Especially at lunch.

Well, apparently, teachers had noticed this too, which was why we all got stuck with this new program, twice a week, called Stir-It-Up Lunch, which is as horrible as it sounds. Everybody draws a colored slip of paper, and that determines which lunch table you sit at twice a week FOR THE WHOLE YEAR. They don't even sort you by grade. Henry and I landed at the Blue Table, with a bunch of little kids. The worst was this first-grade boy named Rodney, who still wiped his nose on his sleeve.

"Rodney," I kept saying. "Do you want a Kleenex?"

"No."

Henry looked at me and shook his head sadly. "So gross," he said. Rodney could hear him too, but he didn't even seem to mind.

"I'm losing my appetite," I said to Henry.

Henry didn't answer. He was busy arranging each part of his lunch on top of his lunch bag. Cheese sandwich, carrot sticks, granola bar. I didn't know it yet, but that was Henry's standard lunch. And by "standard," I mean that he ate it every day for the whole school year as far as I could tell. Not only that, but he ate it in the same order every time and finished each item before he moved on to the next. He's one of those kids who won't let any of the food touch on his dinner plate.

Somewhere between the last carrot stick and the granola bar, Rodney sniffed so loudly that it was really more of a snort. The littler kids at the table thought it was hilarious, but Henry and I had had enough.

"We need to get out of here," he told me.

And that's how it started. Henry and I would take a few

bites, then hide the rest of our lunch in a jacket pocket and escape to the playground. Nobody else was outside yet, so we just started sitting together, sharing cookies under the slide. We didn't even talk much, which is unusual for me. We just sat there chewing and staring at the wood chips. Once I had finished, I'd dust myself off and get up to go find someone I knew.

"Bye, Henry," I'd say.

And he would nod and take out his sketchbook. That's how it went for a few weeks. Henry and I left every Stir-It-Up Lunch early, and the rest of the Blue Table just watched us go.

Eventually, of course, somebody caught on. The somebody in this case was Mr. Simmonds, the new science teacher. It was his first year at Washington Carver too, which was probably why he had lunch duty all the time. Anyway, he stuck his head under the slide one Monday afternoon and demanded to know what Henry and I were doing. And the way he asked made it sound like we were doing something way worse than finishing a bologna sandwich.

"If you aren't done with lunch," he told us, "you belong inside, where you can be properly supervised."

How much supervision do you need to eat a bologna sandwich? That is what I was thinking. What I said, luckily, was nothing. But what I did was sigh loudly and roll my eyes, and I'm pretty sure that's what sank us.

We got sent inside, but not back to the cafeteria. We had to go all the way down the hall to the principal's office. We had to sit side by side waiting for him—Boris Borkowski, a huge bald man with a temper. More-fortunate kids were leaving the office with their parents—heading home with the stomach flu or on their way to have some painful dental procedure. I envied all of them.

Simmonds went in ahead of us to describe our crime in private. Then he motioned us into the office and left us there to face Mr. Borkowski alone.

"Do either of you know what the term 'in loco parentis' means?" Borkowski asked.

Henry and I looked at each other, confused. Great. Now, on top of everything else, we were about to fail some pop quiz on weird vocabulary words.

I got nervous, so I guessed. "Crazy parents?" I asked.

"No!" said Borkowski. "What it means, in short, is that for the duration of the school day, we are responsible for you. Ethically, morally, *legally* responsible."

Henry and I just blinked and nodded.

"And it is very difficult for us to live up to that responsibility if students take it upon themselves to vanish in the middle of the school day."

I was trying hard not to smile. It's something that

happens when I get really nervous. Even worse, I felt like I might laugh. Fortunately, I was able to turn it into a pretty convincing fake cough, and Borkowski let me go around the corner for a drink of water.

When I got back, Henry was saying, "You really shouldn't blame Barbara Anne. It was my idea. She was just being nice."

I stared at him and opened my mouth to say something, but Henry kicked me in the shin. And Borkowski's desk was so big that he didn't even see it. Henry got away with it and kept on going with his speech. "And really," he said. "Isn't that the whole purpose of this new program? To help students meet people and make new friends?"

Wow. Henry was really laying it on thick. Borkowski stared at him for a minute. And during that pause, the phone rang. And whoever or whatever it was, it was more important than the two of us sneaking out of the cafeteria.

"I don't want to see the two of you in here again," Borkowski said as he waved us out of the office. I'm not sure he even heard Henry promising that we'd stay in the cafeteria from now on.

"Thanks," I told Henry as we headed back down the hall. "That was really brave of you."

"No," he said. "I was terrified."

"Of what he would do to us?" I asked.

"No," Henry said. "Of what you would say if I gave you a chance to talk again."

And that was the thing about Henry. Most of the time, he was so quiet that he seemed like this ordinary, almost boring kid, but then he would surprise you. I guess the same was true, in a way, about everyone in our pod. There was a lot I didn't know about them at the start of the year. And each one of them was keeping a secret. I just happened to figure out Henry's first.

For weeks, Henry spent almost every recess off by himself, drawing. He wouldn't show me what he was working on. But there he would be, every day, off in the same corner, knees drawn up, head bent over his sketchbook. Curiosity was killing me, of course, but I didn't ask. I'm kind of proud of that. I've been working on "giving people space," to use my mother's words. She says my energy can overwhelm people. So I waited it out, and one day he just laid the sketchbook down in the open space between us. And there he was: Edgar. Henry's ghost.

I suppose you're picturing some Ebenezer Scrooge sort of situation now. You know, some ancient guy in gauzy robes, hollow eyes, dragging chains. That sort of thing. But you'd be wrong. For one thing, this ghost was just a kid. If it weren't for the weird, old-fashioned clothes, he could have walked right into Ms. Biniam's fifth-grade class with the rest of us, and nobody would even have noticed.

"Who is he?" I asked Henry when he showed me the drawing.

"It doesn't matter," Henry said. "He isn't real."

"Oh," I said. "You mean you just made him up?"

"No," Henry said. "I've seen him. But he isn't real; he isn't really there."

My first thought was that Henry had an imaginary friend, but, I mean, who has an imaginary friend in the fifth grade? "Henry," I said. "You're talking in riddles."

"I don't know who he is," Henry said. "Or who he *was*." His voice got kind of shaky, and his chin began to wobble. "All I know," Henry said, "is that he follows me. Everywhere."

CHAPTER TWO

THE OUIJA BOARD

The next day, as we were standing in line for gym class, Henry leaned forward and whispered in my ear. His breath tickled, and his voice was so low that I couldn't understand a word he was saying. I shrugged at him and made a *What?* face, so he tried again.

"That thing I told you yesterday," he said. "Forget it."

"Oh," I said, probably louder than I should have. Henry glared at me, so I started again, more quietly. "You mean about your gho—good friend?"

"Yes," said Henry. "Can you just pretend I never mentioned it?"

Well, that would be impossible. As soon as I realized that

Henry was dealing with a ghost, I knew we had to do something. But Henry wasn't too excited about my plan.

"Henry," I said. "You can trust me. We're friends. And I know what I'm doing."

Henry still looked skeptical, so I added, "It'll be fun. You'll see."

None of that was exactly, technically true. I had no idea what I was doing, and he had no reason to trust me. Henry and I didn't even know each other all that well. We were friendly, sure. We sat next to each other all day. And I had gone over to his house once after school, but I'd pretty much invited myself. Still, I did know enough about Henry to understand why he wasn't excited about my idea. Henry didn't even like to talk to live people that much, so why would he want to speak to a dead one? But here's the thing about me. Once I think I have the answer to something, nothing can stop me.

Getting the Ouija board was easy. I knew there was one in my cousin Monica's closet underneath a big pile of games like Candy Land that none of us played anymore. And Monica doesn't care what you take from her closet as long as it isn't her clothes. (She has made it very clear that I don't get to borrow those—even though I know for a fact that some of them would fit, and most of them would look great on me.) The only hard part of holding our séance, or Ouija board thing, actually, was dealing with Alice—Henry's younger sister. She's a pain.

Alice wants to be a ballerina. She goes around all the time in one of those tiny little ballerina buns; it's like a little blond knob at the top of her head. Henry says she takes lessons twice a week, and she even has this tiny toy mouse with a tutu that she calls Miss Nibbles. It's a big emergency every time she loses the thing, which, according to Henry, happens pretty often.

Okay. I'll admit that the first time I was over there, we straight-out hid it from the kid. It wasn't right, but it was hilarious. Miss Nibbles hanging halfway out the window. Miss Nibbles dangling over a pot of chili.

"Henry," Sophie said. "Have you seen your sister's mouse?"

"No," Henry answered. Straight face. Not even a hint of a smile. I was so proud of him.

"Well, could you at least look?"

I'm pretty sure the little stuffed rodent was in Henry's pocket the whole time while we went around the house calling, "Miss Nibbles! Miss Nibbles!"

Sophie glared at Henry.

"What?" he asked. "You wanted us to help. We're helping."

Henry's always really polite to everyone else. I guess his stepmother just doesn't bring out the best in him.

Of course, I wanted to use the Ouija board the second I got it, but because of Alice (whose favorite sentence is "I'm telling!"), Henry and I had to wait a couple of days. Until Alice had a ballet lesson. Those were the only days Henry had the house to himself—for a little while—until Sophie got home from work.

I never had the house to myself because that's what happens when your dad works from home some days and your baby sister is an actual baby. All you can do is put a KEEP OUT sign on your bedroom door and hope for a few minutes' peace when everyone falls asleep—Rachel in her crib, and Mom and Dad on the couch in front of the news. That's when I get the rest of the pizza to myself and a bit of privacy. Henry didn't know how lucky he was. So, while Alice was off learning how to put her feet in second position, we went to Henry's house.

As soon as we got there, I started to set things up.

"We have exactly one hour to finish. One hour until Sophie gets home from work."

"Okay, okay," I said. "I understand."

"If we were at my mom's house, it would be different, but Sophie just . . ."

"It's all right, Henry," I said. "What's your mom doing in England, anyway?"

"Studying Shakespeare," Henry said. "Uncle Marty told me she's writing about ghosts."

His answer surprised me so much that I just stared at him for a second. Then I said, "We'd better hurry."

Henry had no idea what to do with a Ouija board, so he really should have been more cooperative.

"What are you doing?" he asked me as I closed the living room curtains.

"Making it darker."

"How are we supposed to see the board?" Henry complained.

"Have you got any candles?" Honestly, sometimes he has no imagination.

"We don't need any candles. Just leave the stupid curtains open."

"Henry," I said. "Do you want this to work or not?"

"Fine. But at least leave them open a crack."

It ruined the whole mood, but it was hard to refuse him. If you could have seen how nervous he looked, you'd understand.

We put the Ouija board in the center of the coffee table and sat crisscross applesauce on the living room floor.

"Spirits, are you here?" I asked. "Make yourselves known!"

"What's wrong with your voice?" Henry asked.

"That's how you do it!" I said.

"Says who? Your Ouija board teacher?"

"Do *you* want to do it?" I asked him.

"No," Henry said. "I want you to do it. In your regular voice."

"Stop wasting time," I said. "Put your fingers on the edge of the planchette."

"The *planchette*?" he asked.

"Yes. That's what it's called. And don't push it! You just touch it lightly. Spirits, are you—" But I never finished because we both felt it: the disk lurched toward the corner of the board, to the small circle that said YES.

"Who are you?" Henry demanded.

And it happened again. Five times, to be exact. Once for each letter: E-D-G-A-R.

And just like that, Henry's ghost had a name.

CHAPTER THREE

THE FAMOUS FOX SISTERS

I suppose it's possible you don't believe me. Even now. Maybe you're thinking Henry and I are just two kids making up some game to scare ourselves. Like that time my cousin Monica and I went to Girl Scout camp, and everyone charged out of the cabin in the middle of the night, screaming, so sure they'd just seen Mary Worth in the bathroom mirror. Mrs. Sorenson was standing there, in a flannel pajama top and sweatpants, yelling, "If you girls don't want to settle down, we can just load up the vans RIGHT NOW and head home!" Immediately everybody got really quiet—which I don't understand, because it was so obvious that she wasn't going to do anything until she had a full night's sleep and at least two cups of coffee. P.S. We got to stay until the next day, when they told us to "forage" for our breakfast, which turned out to be miniature boxes of cereal hanging from the nearest trees. This is supposed to teach us to survive in nature? Seriously? Not much of a camper, that Mrs. Sorenson.

But just because the Mary Worth thing was a big fat fake doesn't mean something didn't happen that day with Henry and me. Lots of people have held séances with Ouija boards. You can look it up. Once, a really long time ago, there were these two sisters called Maggie and Kate Fox. They lived in a farmhouse in New York, and they wanted to scare their parents, so they started making ghost noises in the middle of the night. They tied apples together and bounced them along the floor to make it sound like footsteps. They taught themselves to make loud snapping sounds with their toes, which isn't easy. I've tried it.

Anyway, once their mother heard the noises, she was completely convinced the farmhouse was haunted. She just got up out of bed, lit a candle, and started searching for ghosts. That's when Maggie and Kate started to think that maybe they'd gone too far. They tried to say that it was almost April Fools' Day, and maybe someone was playing a joke. *Hint, hint, hint.* But it was too late. The whole thing had gotten out of hand. Before they knew what hit them,

Maggie and Kate were conducting séances for money. They had to learn how to snap their toes with shoes and socks on, but I suppose it was worth it. I bet it paid a lot better than collecting chicken eggs.

I guess when I read about those two, I might have taken it as a warning to slow down on the whole Edgar thing. But I didn't. I couldn't. Edgar wasn't a game. He wasn't a trick that Henry was playing on me. Even if Henry didn't always want to admit it, Edgar was real. And he kept showing up.

One day after school, I was at Henry's house, playing catch in the yard. It wasn't our first choice, but Sophie said we should go outside, and I figured Henry could use the practice. Not that he appreciated my efforts. At all.

"You have to stand sideways," I told him. "Sideways and shift. That's what my dad says."

"It doesn't matter where my feet are," Henry said. "This isn't dance class, Barbara Anne. It's about my arm."

I was sincerely hoping that wasn't true, because Henry had an arm like an overcooked spaghetti noodle. And he wasn't any better at catching than he was at throwing. Every ball I threw escaped him. Even when I threw *right* to him, Henry kept missing. It was like his mind was a million miles away. The ball sailed past him and rolled toward the bushes at the edge of the yard so many times that I quit helping him search for it.

I sat down in the grass instead. And when Henry got back, he joined me. "What's up with you?" I asked him.

"I saw him," Henry said.

"Just now?" I asked.

"No," Henry said. "Last night. It's getting worse. It happens all the time now." And that's when Henry told me that the night before, Edgar had shown up in his room. "He was right there," Henry said. "Standing at the foot of my bed—by the window. He had this brown wooden yo-yo. And he was doing tricks with it. The one my grandfather used to do where you hook your fingers through the string and form this opening. Then the yo-yo just hangs there in the center, swaying."

"Rock the Baby," I told him.

But Henry wasn't listening.

"He looked right at me!" Henry said. "His voice was all breathy and strange."

"You talked to him? What did he say?"

Henry turned to me, his eyes creepy and wild; he grabbed my hand really tightly in his own.

"What did he say?" I asked again.

Instead of answering right away, Henry started lacing our fingers together. Then he looked off into the distance like he was watching a movie that only he could see. When he finally looked at me again, he had those strange, scary eyes. *"Play with me!"* Henry said.

And I screamed. Not an *Oh no, I'm about to be tagged on the playground* scream. An actual full-out scream that scraped against the back of my throat. That's how real Edgar was, even for me. And I'd never seen him.

CHAPTER FOUR

THE NIGHT OF THE PLAY

At school, Henry had to face another sort of horror because we had a new class project: the school play.

"Everyone in the fifth grade gets a part," Ms. Biniam said. "I expect one hundred percent participation!"

Usually, you want to be in a play. You have to audition to get a part, and it's super exciting when they post the cast list. But this was as voluntary as a fire drill, and from the very first second it went badly. And it did not help that we lost our afternoon recess almost every day to make time for the rehearsals.

"I'm organizing a strike," Henry said as we were waiting backstage, hidden behind a cardboard castle. Renee was up on a stepladder because she was Rapunzel.

"You can't organize a strike," I said. "This is Biniam's favorite assignment all year. She said so."

"Well, I'm not going onstage in that costume she gave me," Henry said.

"Be quiet!" Renee hissed at us. "I need to hear my cue."

"Rapunzel, Rapunzel! Let down your golden hair," Ms. Biniam said.

"Why is Biniam reading the lines? Where's the prince?" Henry asked.

"Had to go home," I said. "I heard he has lice."

"Every time I hear that word, my head starts to itch," Henry said.

"Rapunzel, RAPUNZEL!" said Ms. Biniam.

"See," Renee said. "You made me miss my part."

"You know that doesn't make any sense," Henry said. "Obviously her hair is not golden. It's brown."

"Maybe they'll give her a wig," Zack said. "A wig full of lice!"

"Shut up, Zack!" Renee said.

"Don't worry about it, Renee," I said. And then I stepped out from behind the castle.

"What's going on back there?" Ms. Biniam asked.

"We were thinking he should say, 'Let down your beautiful hair.' You know, since Renee has brown hair."

"Fine," said Ms. Biniam. "Let's continue with the rehearsal."

"I don't care what she says," Henry was saying behind the castle. "I'm not wearing it. There's no way."

I sighed and went out to talk to Ms. Biniam again.

"Also," I said. "Henry is really unhappy about his costume. Just so you know."

"Henry's costume is already sewn. And that is the costume that Henry will be wearing. Just so *you* know," said Ms. Biniam.

I was speechless. Ms. Biniam had never talked to me that way. Ms. Biniam, who is so beautiful she looks like an Ethiopian princess, and so kind that kids look forward to having her as their teacher for years. Years! I just stared at her, neither of us saying anything. And then we heard the fight break out backstage.

"Maybe I already know my lines!" Zack was yelling.

"You don't even HAVE real lines," Renee said. "You're an ogre! All you have to do is stomp and grunt."

"What are you laughing at, Henry?" Zack screamed.

And that's when the castle tipped and collapsed with a thud. Renee shrieked, Henry laughed harder, and Ms. Biniam closed her eyes and started to rub the bridge of her nose. "Line up at the door," she told us. "Twenty-minute recess."

Things got even worse during dress rehearsal. Because of the costumes. Since Ms. Biniam changed the part about the golden hair, Renee did not have to wear a wig.

"You saved my life, Barbara Anne!" she told me. After that, she acted like we were best friends or something.

Renee got to wear her real hair, braided, of course, and this pale blue princess dress that was basically the best costume in the whole show.

I did okay too. I was Little Red Riding Hood, so I got to wear a checked dress with a white apron and a shiny red cape. Ms. Biniam painted solid red circles on my cheeks. That part was a little ridiculous, I thought. But other people said I looked adorable, and who was I to argue?

But Henry. Oh wow, Henry did not do well in the costume department. Here's what he had to wear: green velvet shorts with white kneesocks and suspenders. I felt sorry for him. I really did. People were just starting to get to know him, to see the real Henry a little and not the kid in the chess school T-shirt, and Biniam went and dressed him like some leprechaun lost at Oktoberfest. It was an outrage, really.

But it was kind of hard not to laugh too. I managed, but certain people did not have my level of self-control. Renee and Zack? Well, they could hardly contain themselves.

"Zachary!" Ms. Biniam said. "This is dress rehearsal. Show some respect."

"Yes, Ms. Biniam," Zack said. But then he whispered to Renee, "What is he? An elf?"

Biniam heard him. She has amazing hearing. It must be her strongest sense. (Mine is taste.) She is good at everything, really. Except makeup. I'd give her a C, C+ tops, for makeup.

"He is Hansel, Zack. His name is Hansel," Ms. Biniam said.

"I thought his name was Henry," one of the younger kids said.

"His name *is* Henry, sweetheart," one of the volunteer moms said, looking up. And then she pointed to Ms. Biniam to get the kid to pay attention.

"His name is Henry/Hansel, whatever. And your name is Zachary," said Ms. Biniam. "And this is dress rehearsal! And that does not involve talking!"

Before I had time to point out that we would obviously have to speak to perform the play, Ms. Biniam said, "Barbara Anne, that goes for you too."

Man, she was taking this thing seriously. Henry gave us all a smug look because we had gotten in trouble. All because of him and how stupid he looked in his stupid costume. That smirk on his face made me mad. I had a few things I wanted to say, but, fortunately for Henry, I had to go onstage. It was time for me to get fake-eaten by the wolf.

Things were pretty tense in our pod the day of the play. Actually, the whole class was pretty cranky, but I tried not to pay attention to any of it. A good actress has to know how to concentrate. I figured that once the play ended, things would go back to normal. Everyone would congratulate each other on how well we all did, and we would be friends again.

And I was right, in a way. Things went great. For me. I remembered all my lines, and it was really exciting to be on-stage! When I got off, it was Henry's turn to go be Hansel. He looked ridiculous in his green velvet shorts and goofy suspenders. He also looked terrified.

And that is why what happened next happened next. I was afraid he wouldn't go out there at all if I didn't give him a little encouragement.

"Break a leg, Henry," I whispered.

And then I gave him a little push. Not a shove. Just a little gentle nudge, really. I'd call it a nudge. The trouble was that whatever you call it, it was enough to send Henry out onto the stage while his green hat with the feather on top landed just behind the curtain at my feet.

And so I did what you do when somebody drops something. I yelled, "Hey, Henry, you forgot your hat!" And then I walked out and handed it to him. And then I noticed everyone. The audience. It looked like the whole city of Seattle was staring back at us, waiting for something to happen. So I did a quick curtsy before I ran off.

People laughed. And clapped. There were a few whistles, even. And Henry, of course, was mortified. I couldn't see it because of the makeup, but I knew his face was bright red. And the look Henry gave me before the audience stopped laughing! Well, I pretty much figured that my friendship with Henry was over.

When I got offstage after the show, I didn't know how to feel. Everyone was there: my mom; my dad; my baby sister, Rachel; my grandmother; my cousin. It was a nice turnout. They were all telling me how great the play was, and it would have been the best time ever except that all I could think about was what happened with Henry. His family was there too, so I asked my mom if I could go over and say hello, and I got just-for-a-minute permission.

"Henry was really great in the play," I told his stepmom. Because everyone likes to get a compliment. Also, I was hoping they weren't mad at me about the whole thing with the hat.

"Where did they get that costume?" Alice asked.

"Alice," Henry's father said in a serious voice (and he gave her a warning look). Sophie put her hand on Alice's shoulder. Alice is such a stepmother's pet. Is that a thing? I'm pretty sure it is. And I'm pretty sure that if you look it up in the dictionary, Alice's picture is in there.

"We should get going," Sophie said to Henry's father over the top of my head.

"Nice to see you," I said. "Have you seen Henry?"

Henry came up then in his outfit/costume. I was just about to tell him how great he was in the play when, despite all warnings, Alice burst out laughing. Maybe she felt safe because Sophie was standing behind her. But this is the surprising thing that Sophie said: "Alice, stop. You should be very proud of your brother. It takes real courage to get up onstage and perform for a live audience."

"Especially if you're wearing *that!*" Alice said. She was hooting like an owl.

"That's enough," Henry's dad told her. "Let's get going. It's getting late," he said to the whole family.

"I forgot my backpack," Henry said. He seemed embarrassed. I wanted to apologize so badly, but Henry wouldn't even look at me.

"Go get it," his dad said. "I'll pull around out front."

Henry was miserable, and I couldn't blame him. His whole family and most of the school had just watched him humiliate himself in green velvet shorts. And, without meaning to, I had made it even worse. I had to explain. I had to talk to him.

That's why I followed Henry.

The hallway was packed with people, and outside the rain was coming down so hard you could hear it hitting the glass of the windows and doors. People were dashing to their cars, crouched under their coats and huddled together under too-tiny umbrellas. "Wow," someone said as they opened a side door of the school. "It's really coming down out there, isn't it?" But I wasn't worried about the rain; my mind was on Henry. And I kept my eyes on him as we wove through the crowd.

And that's when things started to get strange fast. First, Henry walked right past his locker. And so I walked right past too. I guess you could say that I was borderline spying on him at this point. I'll admit it. When I turned my head and looked back at the gym, I could see my parents and my grandmother still talking to people. Well, I could see my father, anyway, because he's pretty tall. So I decided it would be okay to keep going a bit farther down the hall; I had a little time.

Henry didn't even seem to notice that he had gone too far. He was like a zombie. What was he doing? His parents were waiting outside in the car. I couldn't figure it out with my brain, and it was hard to see it with my eyes too because there were so many people in the way. But then I saw Henry start up the stairs toward the music room. I followed, and as

I went up the stairs, I could hear it. Somebody was up there. Playing the piano.

Henry disappeared into the dark room ahead of me. And when I reached the doorway, I froze. I let my eyes get used to the dark for a minute. I couldn't tell where the music was coming from. It was everywhere. The song was so loud. Loud and fast. It filled the whole room; it bounced off the walls. And the music wasn't the only creepy thing. I wish it had been.

Once my eyes got adjusted, I saw Henry standing *next* to the piano. I'd know him anywhere, even in the dark. But here's the thing: nobody was at the piano. The bench was *completely* empty. So I kept walking forward. I needed to know what was happening. My heart was pounding so hard I could sort of feel it in my ears and my chest both.

"Henry?" I whispered. I guess it was absurd to whisper, really. But I think I was a little scared. Anyway, I expected Henry to turn his head or something, but he did nothing. He just kept staring—at the piano, at the empty bench. And when I got close enough, I could see that the keys of the piano were *moving*. All by themselves. Henry wasn't playing the piano; he was *watching* somebody play it. We both were.

And for the first time, in my head and my heart and my body, I was as terrified as Henry must have been all along.

CHAPTER FIVE

THE TRUNK

Usually, when something exciting or scary happens, all I want to do is talk about it—with whoever is there. Right away too. When I jumped off the diving board at the pool for the first time, I yelled, "Did you see me? Did you see me, Mom?" And the last time my cousin Monica babysat me, and we watched a horror movie, I had plenty to say. "She's not going in there alone, is she?" I wanted to know. And Monica had to shush me and turn up the sound.

But what happened with Henry and me in the music room was different. It felt bigger. Too big to talk about for a while. Maybe we both thought that saying anything about it would make it more real—too real.

The worst part was that we had to go up there, for music

class. A few days after it happened, there we were, sitting in a circle on the floor right next to that piano while the music teacher kept talking about percussion instruments. Henry had a tambourine he was supposed to hit at a specific spot in the song we were learning, and I had a triangle. We were looking at each other across the circle, and we both knew that neither one of us was thinking about the song. And neither one of us would turn our head to look at the piano either.

When the song was finished, the music teacher asked us, "What about this piano?"

"What about it?" Henry asked.

"Well, is *this* a percussion instrument? If I play it—"

Henry's hand shot up, but when she called on him, all Henry did was ask if he could go and get water. And I didn't even bother to ask. I just followed Henry down the stairs and into the hallway below.

"Henry," I asked, "are you okay?"

"I just can't. That room."

"I know," I said. "But we can't avoid it forever."

"We can try," Henry said.

"I just don't understand why it happened," I said.

"I told you," Henry said. "Edgar's following me."

"But why does he come here? Why you? Why now?"

After days of holding it in, it felt good to finally admit what had happened. It would have been even better to have had some answers. But that night, Henry would at least get some clues.

The next day, at lunch, Henry told me about the trunk. You see, Henry hadn't lived in his house for very long. They were barely unpacked before school started. And the night before, I guess, Sophie had decided they should put some boxes up in the attic.

"What's up there?" I asked Henry.

Henry's house is pretty old. I imagined whatever they had up there was way more interesting than our crawl space, which is just packed with stuff like old magazines and golf clubs.

"There were skeletons," Henry said. "Human skulls and—"

"Be serious!"

"Not that much. There's this old trunk, but we couldn't get it open," he said.

"Oh my gosh! How big was it?" I asked. "Henry! We've got to open it!"

"Will you calm down? You're gonna choke on your sandwich."

Now, this was not true.

    A. I was not going to choke.

    B. Mr. Lee would just Heimlich me if I did.

    C. A trunk! A whole trunk! A HUGE trunk.

       Maybe it had gold inside. Maybe it had a

wedding gown. It would be a wrinkly, old
yellow one like a skeleton would wear, but still.

I did settle down eventually, but not because Henry told
me to. People were starting to look over, and I did not want
the whole world staring at us.

"Has Alice got dance practice today?" I asked him.

"Yeah. Why?"

"I'm coming over," I said. "We've got to see what is in
that trunk."

"I'm not sure that's such a good idea," Henry said. "If my
dad couldn't get it open, we won't be able to either. Besides,
we left it up there, and I am not going up in that attic again."

"Don't be so negative," I said. "Where's your sense of
adventure?"

Henry just gave me a look and stuffed a cookie in his
mouth.

"Come on!" I said. "Aren't you curious?"

"Fine. But if this turns out badly, it's your fault."

I was so excited about the trunk that it was hard to concentrate on anything else for the rest of the afternoon. Every
single class dragged by as slowly as one of my dad's stories
about work. But once we were at Henry's house, I wasn't
exactly sure how to start. I knew if I asked Henry, he'd say,

"Let's forget the whole thing." So I had to fake it and pretend I had a plan.

"How do you suggest we get it open?" Henry asked.

"Well, let's just first see if there's a key," I said.

"A key?" Henry asked. "Oh, yeah, why didn't I think of that? You're a genius, Barbara Anne! Just wait right here while I go get the key."

Just to clarify, I knew how stupid I sounded, but somehow I couldn't stop. "There could be a key," I continued. "Did you look? While you were up there?" I could tell from the long pause that he had not, so I forged ahead. "Get a flashlight!" I told him. "We're going back up!"

I was kind of picturing myself in some Statue of Liberty pose, holding the flashlight aloft in one hand. I even had a green shirt on.

Henry was not as enthusiastic. He didn't like heights.

"I suppose by 'we' you mean *me*," he said.

Henry had me there. I didn't like heights either. Or shaky ladders. Or dust. Or the idea of sticking my head into a dark attic when Henry was right there and could do it for me.

"Well . . . ," I said.

"I thought so," Henry said.

"It *is* your house."

This was a pretty good argument, I thought. Every kid alive knows this. Whenever somebody is about to do something that will later get everyone in the group in trouble or, worse, injured, the first question anyone asks is not "Is this a bad idea?" but "Whose house is it?" And the usual rule is that the kid whose house it is gets to make the final call. It goes like this:

Kid #1: "Do you really think we should jump off the garage roof?"

Then there's usually a long pause while their eyes flick from the roof to the grass below.

Kid #2 (after a shrug): "Well, it's your house."

Henry wasn't buying it, but he didn't want to seem like a chicken either, so he got the ladder.

Henry appeared to like ladders even less than heights. "Hold it still!" he kept saying as he went up.

He lifted the square of wood that led to the attic and handed it down to me. The ladder got a little tippy then, and Henry was not too happy. Some things were said about whose idea it was and which of us was being a crybaby. But we got through it.

"Do you see anything?" I asked him.

"Cobwebs," Henry said.

"Nothing else?"

"The boxes Sophie made me shove up here last night. I almost fell off the ladder then too. In case you're interested," Henry said.

I was not.

"What about the trunk?" I asked. "Can you see the trunk?"

"It's huge, Barbara Anne. It's pretty hard to miss."

"Well, is there a key in the lock? A key is super small," I said. "You have to *really* look."

"Gee, thanks for the tip," Henry said.

I could have responded; I had things to say. But sometimes in life you have to be the bigger person. "Fine!" I said. "Just come down, then."

Henry had a cobweb in his hair and a smudge of dirt on the tip of his nose when he landed in the hallway, but I knew better than to laugh.

"What now?" he asked.

"Wait!" I said. "Is it like a combination lock? Like a locker lock? Because we could just try a few combinations."

"Do you have any idea how long that would take?" Henry asked. "You are really bad at math, Barbara Anne."

"Am not," I said.

"Look," Henry said. "It's an old, rusty-looking lock, like something that just fell off a pirate ship."

"Well," I said. "Then we need a rock."

"A rock?"

"A big rock."

Henry's yard was really frustrating. It was full of rocks, but most of them were way too tiny to be any good for our purposes. And they were all lined up in this specific wavy pattern.

"It's supposed to look like water," Henry explained when he saw me staring.

"It's rocks. How can it look like water?"

"It *suggests* water," Henry said. "The shape of it."

I raised an eyebrow but didn't say anything. Nobody wants *you* to say how weird their family is. That's *their* job.

But I felt stuck. How was I supposed to pull one rock out of this yard without leaving an obvious hole that would make the entire thing look like a giant jigsaw puzzle with one piece missing?

"Just do it if you're gonna do it!" Henry said.

"I'm deciding," I said. "Stop rushing me."

Finally I found a good rock. Way back against the edge of the fence, where technically it might be part of the neighbor's yard, but I was not going to quibble now. I showed my prize to Henry. And he sighed. It was a big sigh, like when my mom sits down with an especially large basket of laundry that has to be folded. I think what the sigh said was, *Once again, I would like to point out that we should* really *not be doing this.* I ignored it.

I was thrilled with the rock. I would have kissed it if it had not been covered with dirt. But that is because I'm an optimist, a glass-half-full kind of person. Also, I did not realize yet what was about to happen.

I was the one who found the rock, but once we got inside, Henry was the one who had to go back up and get the trunk down.

"I don't think I can lift this," Henry said.

"You don't have to lift it," I told him. "Just shove it over the edge."

"You have no idea how heavy this is, Barbara Anne. It feels like there's a dead body in here."

We both stopped for a minute then because, really, who knew what was inside? But I, for one, was willing to take my chances.

Now we were both shouting. I was yelling at Henry to shove harder, and he was yelling at me to stand back. And then the trunk slid through the hole and landed with a gigantic thud in Henry's upstairs hallway.

Henry climbed back down the ladder, and the two of us just stood there staring at the trunk for a minute.

"Well," Henry said. "It's not going to open itself." He picked up the rock then. And I have to say that, once he started, Henry really threw himself into the whole bashing thing. He lifted that rock up high like a murderer about to bludgeon his victim, paused for one dramatic second, then let it rip.

Here's the thing about the rock. It was large, which was good. But it was also really sharp and pointed on one side, and that's where the problem came in, because unfortunately, the rock did not land where it was supposed to. And that is what happens when you have the eye-hand coordination of a chess player. Henry aimed for the lock but hit his other hand. And it wasn't good. I'm not sure what was more horrifying—the amount of blood or the way Henry was dancing around screaming. And the carpet in the hallway was beige. Of course it was.

I ran to get a towel. I was yelling, "Henry, it's okay!" which was ridiculous. Of course it was not okay. He was gushing blood.

Fortunately, I am pretty calm in an emergency, and I got first-aid training from the Girl Scouts. I grabbed a little towel from the bathroom, so we could wrap up his hand and apply pressure. I was hoping I wouldn't throw up.

"We can't use that," Henry said. "That's a good towel. Sophie will kill me."

Now, I knew what he meant. My grandmother has little shell soaps by the sink that have been there my entire childhood, and everybody knows that water should not touch them under any circumstances. But this was an emergency, so I grabbed his hand and wrapped it up.

"Look," I said. "Do you want to bleed to death just to save Sophie's stupid towel?"

And then we heard the front door. Sophie and Alice were home. There was no time to clean up or do anything. We were just stuck there like deer in headlights.

Alice made it to the top of the steps first, and she really let loose with a scream. Forget dance. She should consider a wind instrument with that kind of lung power. Sophie was right behind her. "What exactly is going on here?" she asked.

I looked at the hallway, at the blood on the used-to-be-superclean carpet. And Henry's poor, pale face. I felt nervous now, and confused too. The whole thing seemed like such a great idea until Sophie got there. And now . . . well, now there was nothing to do but try to make the best of it and hope Henry wouldn't get in too much trouble after I left.

"As you can see," I said, "Henry's had a little accident. And I was just applying some pressure to the wound."

Sophie looked unconvinced. She was not buying it. Henry and I exchanged a look.

It *had* gone badly. It was all my fault.

And now we would never even know what was inside the trunk.

Five stitches. That was the damage. If you don't count whatever it cost to visit the ER and pay to clean the carpet. I wasn't thinking of those things, but my mother was kind enough to point them out to me after she got off the phone with Sophie that night. I was more worried about my friendship with Henry.

But he seemed pretty okay with it the next day. I mean, his hand was all bandaged up, but at school any injury that needs more than a Band-Aid is kind of a prize. Everybody circles around you and wants to know what happened. People want to sign your cast. They volunteer to carry your backpack. Getting hurt makes you a minor celebrity, as long as you don't get too whiny about it.

"Did you cry?" Zack wanted to know as we settled down into our pod of desks at school the next day.

"Of course he didn't cry," I answered for him.

And Zack gave a little nod. It was the first hint of respect he'd shown Henry all year. "Wow," he said. "Five stitches."

Henry looked kind of proud of himself then. And when we got outside after lunch, he had something to show me. Apparently, after I'd left, Henry's dad had used a crowbar to pry open the trunk. And now, zipped inside Henry's backpack, was a pile of gray and cream-colored cardboard and paper.

"What's this?" I asked. I was already pulling it out—a photograph in a cardboard frame. And there he was: Edgar, the same boy from Henry's sketches, smiling out at me from the front porch of Henry's house. I felt a shiver go through me, because I knew right then that Edgar would be back. "Henry," I whispered. "You're living in a haunted house."

CHAPTER SIX

GHOST HUNTERS

I knew Henry and I couldn't count on any more facts about Edgar just landing with a crash at our feet. If we wanted to know more, we had to get serious—like those ghost hunter guys on TV. I was planning on watching them after school with Henry, but he had to go to the dentist, so I asked Renee. To be honest, I was lucky to be watching them with anyone. My mom is not a big fan of television. She calls it "screen time" when I'm around and "the idiot box" when she thinks I'm not listening. I think you get the picture. But she was in an especially good mood that day. She even let us get cake pops when she stopped for coffee. And usually if I ask for anything sweet, all I get is a lecture about sugar, aka "the white death."

Anyway, when we sat down in the den, I knew what I wanted to watch. But in my house, the rule is "Be nice to your guest." I mean, it's not like it's stitched into a pillow or hanging as a sign on the wall, but that's the rule. So I let Renee pick first. Big mistake.

Renee has the worst taste in shows ever. The one she wanted was just ladies trying on wedding gowns. They would stand on this little round stage that looked like the top of a cake and twirl around. And their moms and friends would start crying—actually crying!—and saying stuff like, "Oh, Tracy. You look so beautiful. I just wish your father was here to see you."

"I'm never getting married," I announced.

"Why?" Renee asked. "You get to dress up like a princess, and everybody gives you gifts. And money. You get a lot of money."

"They don't even show the guy she has to marry," I pointed out. "Or the girl."

"That's not the point."

"But maybe he's awful," I said. "Did you ever think about that?"

Renee ignored me. She was staring at the screen like someone had hypnotized her.

"I don't have to wait that long anyway," Renee said. "My grandmother's gonna make me an amazing dress for my *quinceañera.*"

"What's that?"

"My fifteenth birthday party," Renee said. "I might get a tiara too."

"That sounds great," I said, but I guess she could tell from my voice that I couldn't take another minute of the squealing and the twirling.

"You can change it," she said. "If you want to watch something else."

She was pouting a little, so maybe she thought I wouldn't do it, but I grabbed the remote and changed the channel as fast as I could. I flipped past the news and a soap opera and landed on the show I was looking for. This time, they were investigating a haunted hospital. Now, I ask you, what would you rather do: tour an abandoned insane asylum or watch some people you don't even know go shopping? I think the answer is pretty obvious, but Renee started saying, "Switch it back! This is too scary!"

I had to shush her so I could hear the ghost hunter guy.

"We're here, just outside the former Edmonds Institute for the Criminally Insane," he said. "The rest of the team has gone ahead."

He tried to contact them with some crackly walkie-talkie. Then they switched to the other ghost hunters. (The guys who were filming were obviously better at catching ghosts than working cameras. They kept getting so close to people's faces that you could see right up their nostrils. So gross!)

"We're in the East Wing," ghost hunter guy number two said.

The ghost team was lugging bags of equipment and looking really wide-eyed and freaked out. "I've set up the temperature gauges," he whispered. "And the EMF meter. Now we just have to wait."

He paused, and the girl who was with him said the date and time. She wrote it down in a notebook, and I made a mental note to get a notebook. I would have written it down, of course, but I didn't have the notebook yet.

"What's that?" the guy asked all of a sudden.

"I think we need to head this way," the girl told him.

She had a headlamp, like a miner. My dad has one of those too, but he's only ever used it for camping. And once he put it on and grabbed some tweezers because my little cousin stuck a toy sponge up her nose to see if it would fit.

"This is way too scary," Renee said.

I had the basic idea, ghost hunter–wise, so I switched the channel. Anyway—and I say this just to be completely honest—I was hanging out with Renee only because Henry was busy that day. Henry had the real clues. Henry had the stuff he'd found in the trunk.

It seemed like my house was the best place for Henry and me to go through everything because we'd had enough trouble with Sophie already. And the best time, of course, was when my dad was away on a business trip, my mom was out running errands, and my grandmother was babysitting. My grandmother is not as quick with the "What are you two doing?" questions as my parents.

So I told Henry to bring all the Edgar stuff over to my house.

"Stop telling me what to do," he said. "You're so bossy."

"I am not bossy," I said.

Honestly, how come everybody always says that about girls? My grandmother says I'm going to run the world someday, and I'm pretty sure she means it in a good way. Anyway, Henry did what I told him to do and brought the stuff to my house, and my grandmother put out some almond cookies for us. Henry was all ready to take the pictures and stuff out of his backpack when my grandmother started to get a *little* too interested. "What you got there?" she asked.

"Just some stuff," Henry said. "Barbara Anne asked me to bring it over."

"Huh," my grandmother said, which sounds like it means nothing if you don't know my grandmother but means a lot if you do. It's sort of hard to explain.

"Let's take our homework into my room, where we can work on it quietly," I said to Henry.

"Why don't you two eat your cookies right here at the table?" my grandmother said.

"You know," I said, being careful to look straight at Henry and not at my grandmother, "my mother doesn't even let me *have* cookies after school. Isn't my grandmother SWEET to let us have some?"

"Bitsy," my grandmother said. "Watch your step."

Things got a little tense for a minute—not really scary, more like in between a staring contest and you're about to get sent to your room. And then Rachel saved the day by crying, and my grandmother had to go change her diaper.

"What's the matter with you?" Henry asked. "You should be nicer to your grandmother."

"I *am* nice to my grandmother. She's my favorite person on planet Earth. Grab your backpack," I said. "And a couple of cookies."

I didn't want to make Henry witness a diaper change, so I decided we should skip my room and just use my dad's office. Once we were there and Henry started to unzip the backpack, I was so excited I could have peed my pants. All I had seen so far was the one picture Henry managed to show me at recess before the bell rang. Now I got to see the whole stash.

I guess I should tell you that Edgar wasn't alone in the picture. He was standing on the porch with an older boy and two grown-ups. They looked kind of sad and serious, the way most people do in old photographs. I guess nobody smiled much back in the day. Maybe secretly they all knew they were alive too soon and were missing all the good stuff, like television and video games.

"Who do you suppose they are?" I asked Henry.

"Must be his parents, I guess," Henry said.

That wasn't necessarily true. A really good detective would start with a more open mind. I mean, look at Henry. His mom was off in England studying, and he was stuck here with Sophie.

"Maybe," I said. "But you never know. You don't live with your mom right now. And Renee just has her dad and that ancient babysitter lady."

"That's her grandmother, Barbara Anne," Henry said.

"Are you sure?" I asked him. "Maybe her dad's just really bad at picking babysitters."

Henry gave me a look then. He acts like he's never said anything even the least little bit mean about anybody, but that just isn't true. "What else is there?" I asked.

There was so much more: another photo—of a boy and a man standing in front of a piano—a letter, a locket, and a strange little book.

"Let's read the letter first," I said.

"Don't grab it!" Henry said.

And, to be fair, I guess he was right. The paper was so thin it felt more like a leaf than regular paper, and the handwriting was this small, extra-fancy cursive that took some time to get used to. We had to unravel it a little at a time.

My dear Thomas,

You are right to do what you can to prepare now for the coming eventualities. I wish I could be more optimistic, but I share your belief that this illness will reach the farthest corners of the country before it has run its course. It seems a new breed of pneumonia more vicious than any I saw in my civilian practice.

There are ten times the number of doctors that would normally be on base, and even that is not enough as we lose those, and nurses too, at an appalling rate. Each time I take up my stethoscope and hear the rales, I know it is certainly a death sentence, and a rapid one at that. Within hours, the dark spots appear. Cyanosis. Suffocation. As horrible a death as any they could have experienced in France.

"What's he talking about?" I asked Henry.

"I'm not sure," Henry said.

"How's the homework coming?" my grandmother asked from the doorway.

And Henry and I both jumped. Henry stuffed the letter back into his backpack and scrambled to his feet.

"You scared us to death!" I yelled at my grandmother.

"Sorry," she said with a shrug. "Slipper feet. Henry, would you like to stay for dinner?"

"Henry and I aren't even finished eating the delicious almond cookies you brought over," I said.

"You shouldn't be eating in here," my grandmother said. Then she sighed. "Just keep the crumbs off the floor. This is your father's office, you know."

"Oh, I know," I said.

Henry elbowed me. "Thank you for the cookies," he told my grandmother.

That night, at dinner, all I could think about while I pushed the green beans around my plate was the letter inside Henry's backpack. He was sitting right beside me, and I couldn't even talk to him about the only important thing there was to talk about. Instead, I had to listen to my mother asking him stupid questions just to make conversation. I mean, who really cared if he'd gotten his hair cut?

"You two don't seem very hungry," my mother said. "Did they serve something great for lunch at school today?"

"We didn't get much homework," I said.

"Earth to Bitsy," my grandmother said.

"Mom," my mom said.

"I'm fine," I said. "Just thinking about homework, I guess."

"Well, now that you mention it, we better get Henry home so you can get started," my mom said.

"After we get back, maybe you can help us with the dishes," my grandmother said.

"I can handle the dishes," my mom said.

"Thanks, Mom," I told her. "You're the best."

My grandmother rolled her eyes, but my mother didn't see it, so that was the end of that round. It isn't nice to keep score, but I think we all know who won.

My idea was that I would walk Henry home by myself, but my grandmother insisted she should come with us. She said it was for safety, but I think she also wanted to know what we were up to.

"It's getting dark, Bitsy," my mom said. "Your grandmother should go along."

"Yeah, *Bitsy*," Henry said. "Your mom's right." He was smirking at me, and I did not like it one bit.

"Very funny," I told him. "Just get your jacket. And I want the little book, okay? If you work on the letter, I'll take a look at the book."

My grandmother walked in as Henry was handing it to

me, and she gave me a curious look. "Just homework," I said. I kissed Rachel on the top of the head, and then we left.

Technically, my grandmother was walking with Henry and me, but she doesn't walk all that fast. The closer we got to Henry's house, the wider the gap became. On the corner across from his house, though, Henry slowed, then stopped. At first, I thought he was just waiting for my grandmother to catch up so the three of us could cross together. But then I saw that he was staring at his house—at his own bedroom window, to be exact.

I swear to you that there was nothing there. The lights weren't even on. But it seemed like Henry saw something, or someone, up in the dark window of his room. I looked up again, but I couldn't make out anything. And I guess I shouldn't have tried. I guess I should have been paying attention.

"Henry!" I screamed when I saw the car.

I remember the red of the brake lights and the loud screech of the tires.

Henry froze right there in the middle of the street. The car missed him by inches, and he didn't even seem upset. He just stood there with this strange, blank look on his face as the headlights washed over him. Then the lady in the car rolled her window down. "I'm so sorry," she said to my grandmother, who was by Henry's side now. "I didn't see him. He came out of nowhere."

"It's all right," my grandmother said, more to Henry than the lady.

Henry himself said exactly nothing—not then, not ever. He didn't have to. I knew who Henry saw in the window that night, and I was more afraid of Edgar than ever.

CHAPTER SEVEN

PROMISE NOT TO TELL

It's funny how things work out. If Henry hadn't been absent that day, Zack and Renee might never have known about Edgar. As it was, though, Henry's secret didn't last until lunchtime. It was true that in all the weeks I'd known about Edgar, I'd never once said a word about him to anyone but Henry. But after that near miss with the car, I was worried, and even Zack could tell something was up.

We were supposed to be doing a group project. Building our container for the egg drop contest. And Renee and Zack were having this huge fight about how to design it.

"The box has to be bigger," Zack said. "So we can fit in more stuff to cushion the egg."

"The bigger you make it, the heavier it gets!" Renee said.

"That's just going to make it land harder and crack even more."

"That's why we stuff the box!" Zack said.

"We need Henry," Renee said. "Henry would know what to do."

"I know what to do," Zack said. "Just help me stuff it."

"Stuff it yourself!" Renee said. "I quit!"

"How come *you're* not helping?" Zack asked me. "You've been acting weird all morning."

"I'm worried about Henry."

"Biniam says he's got bronchitis," Renee said.

"It's not that," I said.

Renee and Zack were staring at me then. "Never mind," I told them.

"Listen," Zack said. "If something's wrong with Henry, we want to know too."

I shook my head. "No," I said. "I really shouldn't. I told Henry I wouldn't say anything."

"Give us a hint," Renee said.

"Did he get in trouble for something?" Zack asked.

"Henry?" I asked. "He never does anything wrong. He says 'excuse me' when he bumps into the pencil sharpener."

"Oh, just spill it!" Zack said.

I know I shouldn't have. I know I promised not to. But I couldn't stand it anymore. "His house is haunted, okay?" I yelled at them, a little louder than I meant to.

"What?" Zack asked.

"Oh no!" Renee said. "Is that why you've been watching all those shows? Those ghost hunter shows?"

"That's ridiculous," Zack said. "My dad says there's no such thing as ghosts. Whenever you hear a story like that, there's a scientific explanation."

"Like what?" I demanded.

"Like carbon monoxide."

"What?"

"Yeah," Zack said. "Carbon monoxide. You can have a leak, and then it poisons you. It causes hallucinations. You can start imagining all sorts of stuff."

"Well, Henry saw something," I insisted. "Up in the window of his room. And it wasn't because of carbon monoxide! He's lucky he didn't get hit by a car. That's how hard he was staring at it."

Biniam came up to our pod then, to check on us. "Making progress?" she asked.

"Yes," Zack said. "Barbara Anne has some really interesting ideas."

But there must have been at least some small part of Zack that was willing to believe me, because instead of running off to play tetherball, he came looking for me on the playground after lunch. "Hey," he said. "What makes you think it was a ghost Henry saw up in the window?"

"Well, for one thing, this isn't the first time it's happened," I told him. "But look, I shouldn't have told you any of this. Henry's going to be really mad. Promise not to tell, okay?"

"About what?" asked Renee as she walked up to join us.

"About Barbara Anne spilling the beans," Zack said.

"Maybe we can help him," Renee said. "He's not going to be mad if we help him get rid of it."

And as soon as she said it, I realized that she might have a point.

"How do we do that?" Zack asked.

"No idea," I told them.

But then, later, during silent reading time, Renee asked, "Do you know anything about him, this ghost?"

"Just his name," I said. "Edgar."

"What?" Zack asked. "He introduced himself?"

"Not exactly," I said. "We used a Ouija board."

"Wow," Renee said. "Did you ask him anything else?"

"Like what?"

"I don't know," she said. "How he died, why he's there, what he wants."

I stared at her for a second. It was such a good list of questions. I almost wanted to write it down. "No," I said. "We didn't think of any of that. I guess we were just so freaked out to get any answer at all."

"He was probably murdered," Zack said.

"You don't have anything to contribute to this conversation," I told him. "You don't even think he's real."

"True," Zack said. "But I still say he was murdered."

"Or, maybe his dad died at sea and he's waiting for him to come back," Renee said. "Oh, maybe he drowned! They didn't give kids swimming lessons back in the day like they do now. Wait! What's he look like?"

"What's the difference?" I asked.

"It's a clue," Renee said. "Like if he's dripping wet or bloody or carrying something strange. Oh! Does he say anything?"

"Well, one time when Henry saw him, Edgar was carrying a yo-yo," I said. "And he asked Henry to play with him."

"Sounds terrifying," Zack said.

I glared at him. "We're trying to figure out more," I said. "We have some stuff. Henry has this letter, this section of a letter, but it's pretty confusing."

"You have a letter written by a ghost?" Renee asked.

"We don't know who wrote it," I said. "It's written to some guy named Thomas, but it isn't signed, and we're not even sure what it's about yet. And we have a book, a sort of scrapbook/yearbook thing. But we're not exactly sure what that means either, or why it was up there."

"Where?" Zack asked.

"In the trunk," I said. "From the attic. At Henry's house. It wasn't easy getting it either. We tried to smash the lock off with a rock. Henry cut his hand wide open."

"That's why he got those stitches?" Renee asked.

I nodded. "His dad got it open later—with a crowbar!"

"Wow," Zack said. And for somebody who didn't believe in ghosts, he seemed pretty curious about the whole thing. "Where's the stuff now? I want to see."

"Henry's got most of it," I said. "But the yearbook thing is in my locker."

"Go get it," Renee said. "I want to see too."

So I fetched it, and we all had a look. It wasn't easy, because every time Biniam came anywhere near our pod, we had to stuff it back into my desk and pretend we were busy reading our books.

"Do you think it belonged to him?" Renee whispered. "Was it Edgar's book?"

"I think so," I said.

But when we flipped through the book, looking for his picture and his name, we didn't find him. These kids were older anyway. Their pictures were just small squares that looked like they'd been cut out of an old newspaper and pasted into the book. I couldn't decide exactly what it was, but there was something creepy about them too. Maybe it was the way the ink had started to fade. They seemed to be looking out at us from a haze or fog. Smiling. Like they knew something that we didn't. They had strange, old-fashioned names, like Evangeline. But we didn't see anyone named Edgar.

"Check inside the front cover," Zack said. "See if there's a name."

And inside the front cover, it said:

This Book Belongs to
P. Winterson

"Look at that," I said. "It's the fanciest cursive writing I've ever seen."

"Biniam's coming!" Zack said. And I hid the book in my desk.

When Biniam came over to our pod, we all thought she was going to yell at us for talking, or ask to see what we'd been looking at, but instead she just said, "Barbara Anne, I was wondering if you might want to take Henry's home-work to him. He might be out for a while."

"Sure," I said, and I reached to grab the folder she was handing me. Then I looked inside Henry's desk to find his math book. And that's the first time it happened. A blue marble rolled out of Henry's desk and onto the floor. I didn't really think much about it that time. I just put it in my pocket, thinking I would give it to Henry later. But I never did. It ended up on my dresser, and I forgot all about it for a while.

I was thinking of other things. On the walk over to Henry's house, I kept wondering if he would be able to tell, right away, that I'd betrayed him. I'm not good at hiding what I'm thinking. Whatever the opposite of a poker face is, that's what I have. I was sort of hoping that Henry would be sleeping when I got there, but no such luck. He was on the couch in the living room watching television. He waved at me as soon as his dad let me in, and he looked so happy to see me that it almost broke my heart.

"Better keep your distance, Barbara Anne," his dad told me. "We don't want you coming down with this too."

"True," I said. "I really just came to drop off the homework."

"Oh, you can stay for a minute," his dad said, and he motioned me to a chair as he started to leave. "Henry probably wants to hear all about what he missed at school today."

That made me gulp. But before Henry could ask me anything, we both spotted them through the window—Zack and Renee, heading toward Henry's front door. Renee had a scraggly-looking bunch of flowers in her hand. I was betting that Zack had ripped them out of someone's yard on the way over.

"Hey, look," Henry said. "It's Zack and Renee."

"What are *they* doing here?" I asked, already beginning to panic.

"I guess they're coming to check on me, same as you," Henry said. He was smiling, but I barely had time to notice. I was already on my way to the door.

"He's fine," I said. "Thanks for coming. I'll take those." I reached for the flowers with one hand and started to close the door with the other.

"Barbara Anne, don't be so rude. Ask them in," Henry said from the couch.

"Yeah, Barbara Anne," said Zack. "Ask us in."

Zack had a smirk on his face, and I whispered to him, "Don't say ANYTHING!"

Renee was even worse. She kept wandering slowly through the room and staring at the ceiling like she expected Edgar to materialize at any moment.

"What's wrong, Renee?" Henry asked.

"Nothing," she said. "I . . . just . . . your house is so . . . interesting."

"Yeah," Zack said. "Not that we know anything about it, but—"

"No," I said. "How could you?"

Henry looked at the three of us, confused for a minute. But Henry is pretty smart, and we weren't fooling him one bit. He let out an exhausted sigh. "Barbara Anne!" he said. "You promised you wouldn't tell."

I said the only thing I could say. "I didn't mean to, Henry. I'm really sorry."

My grandmother was over at my house when I got home, and she took one look at me and asked, "Why so glum, Bitsy?"

"Henry's sick," I said. Of course, I left out the part about what I'd done, and how, sick or well, Henry might not want to spend much time with me in the foreseeable future because of it.

"Oh dear," my grandmother said. "What's wrong with Henry?"

"He has the flu or something," I said.

"Bronchitis," my mother told her, unloading a bag of groceries.

"Same thing," I said.

"It most certainly is NOT the same thing," said my grandmother. "The flu can be very serious. Deadly."

"Who ever died of the flu?" I asked her, grabbing for a cookie.

"Lots of people," she said. "And those are for *after* dinner."

"Of the flu?" I asked. "The flu is like a cold."

"If you're lucky," she said. "When my father was a child, they shut the schools because of the Spanish flu. So many people were dying, they were running out of coffins."

"Mom!" my mother said.

"What? I'm explaining history!" my grandmother said.

"You're scaring your granddaughter," my mother told her. "Honey, Henry has bronchitis, not the Spanish flu. He's going to be just fine. Stop worrying about him and go get started on your homework."

And, of course, my mother was right. Henry did get better—for a while.

CHAPTER EIGHT

HIDE-AND-SEEK

Henry made it back to school just in time for Halloween. You would think he would be celebrating that fact, but Henry hadn't forgotten that I'd told the rest of the pod about Edgar. How could he? Renee kept bringing it up, even though I repeatedly begged her not to. Every other comment from her started with "Can I just ask you one thing?" And then she would want to know "Does he always show up in the same spot?" or "Is he solid, or can you see right through him?" or "Doesn't the rest of your family know he's there?"

And the more she kept asking, the longer Henry stayed mad at me.

"Why did you have to tell them?" Henry asked, more than once.

"I'm sorry," I kept saying. "It just slipped out."

"Just slipped out? How does that even come up in conversation, Barbara Anne? At school? 'What answer did you get for number four, oh, and by the way, did you know Henry's house is haunted?'"

"It just—"

"Never mind," Henry said. "Soon the whole school will know about it, but whatever. It would have been faster to take out an ad on a billboard, Barbara Anne."

And it went on like that. He was really mad. In those moments, he hated me with the same steely concentration my grandmother uses to copy down order numbers off the Home Shopping Network.

And Henry's continued anger wasn't even the only thing I had to face at school. Biniam was threatening to ruin Halloween.

"I'm not saying you can't have fun," she said.

"Here it comes," Zack whispered.

"But it's important to be safe."

This is how it always goes. Before you even make a plan, some adult is telling you why it's too dangerous. It's like some horrible math problem: amount of fun at Halloween =

excitement + sugar + costumes + adventure + friends − (safety rules + parents who won't let you go out alone even in a group of one hundred kids + people who give you an apple or a toothbrush or pocket change because they didn't even remember it WAS Halloween).

Biniam was on the side of the toothbrush people. To be fair, she was paid to be. That's why she started in with the rules on the board. And she did it in the worst possible way—by making us come up with them ourselves, like it was our idea. Classic teacher move. Even I didn't fall for it, and let's face it, my hand is pretty much permanently up in the air.

"Yes, Renee," Ms. Biniam said.

"No masks," Renee said.

"That's a good one. Anything else?" Ms. Biniam asked, all smiles, like she was a waitress offering to bring us pie. "Alonzo?"

"No weapons," Alonzo said.

"Yes! School policy. Good reminder. Would you like to come up and add that to the board?"

Zack looked disgusted. He was leaning back with his hands crossed over his chest. Biniam gave him a look that meant he should stop tipping the chair back on two legs already, but Zack ignored her. Typical. But then he did something really un-Zack-like. He raised his hand.

"Yes, Zachary?" Ms. Biniam asked.

"I don't want to say what I'm going to be, because that would ruin the surprise, but it does have something that comes with it. . . ."

"Okay," Ms. Biniam said slowly. "But remember, right now we're just listing some rules—really just some . . . good reminders, let's say—about how to have a safe Halloween, okay? So let's finish our list."

Zack put his hand down for a while, and the list grew. It was the worst group assignment ever: we were ruining our own Halloween.

When Zack raised his hand a second time, Ms. Biniam called on him before she was even all the way turned around. (It was almost like she had eyes in the back of her head. Which, by the way, would be a GREAT costume.)

"Is this a question, Zachary, or a comment?" she asked.

"A question," Zack said. He looked really indignant, but also confused, like if he didn't spit it out fast, he might completely forget what he wanted to say.

"Go on," said Ms. Biniam.

"Well, an axe is really more of a tool than a weapon," Zack told her.

"No weapons," said Ms. Biniam with a tight smile. "School policy."

That's why it was so hard for the class to come up with our Halloween costumes: nine million rules that we wrote ourselves! At library/computer time, we were allowed to pick a book first or use the computer. Everybody was over by the limit-of-three Halloween books, and that's why I went on the computer first—to this one educational site that the filters don't block. And I found out all about Halloween. Like, for example, did you know that Halloween began a really long time ago as this other holiday (called Samhain)? Well, it did. Like, a really long time ago. Two thousand years. And then they kept changing the name until they finally ended up with Halloween.

And wearing masks? That got started because people believed that spirits returned on Halloween night and wandered the streets. The only safe way to go out into the night was to wear a mask, so the ghosts would mistake you for one of their own. It was basically like a game of ghost/ human hide-and-seek.

It was all pretty interesting. That's why I went to find Henry, to tell him. And also, to see if he would talk to me. But he wasn't at the computers or with the kids who were pulling books from the shelves.

Then I spotted him—all by himself in a big, cushy chair in the corner. He was sitting with his knees drawn up, staring out the window. When I got closer, I could see that he had a sketchbook open on his lap. And it was the weirdest thing. It looked like he was writing, but he wasn't looking down at all. I figured maybe he was just doodling. Or maybe he saw something outside, where the sky was turning gray. A rainstorm was just beginning. As I walked toward Henry, the lights in the library flickered.

"What if the power goes out?" I heard Renee asking the librarian. "Do we get to go home?"

She didn't answer because she was telling everyone to line up. It was time to go back to class. Even if we had no electricity, even if the roof caved in, the schedule would stay the same.

"We have to line up," Renee said. "Tell Henry. Where is Henry?"

"Over there," I said. "Trying to ignore me."

But when I turned to look at Henry again, I started to worry. He was staring right at us, but Henry looked so weird, like he was in some sort of trance.

"What's the matter with him?" Renee asked.

"I don't know," I said.

"Well, you better go get him," Renee said. "He's gonna get in trouble."

I knew Renee was right, but it wasn't as easy as she thought. Henry was in such a daze that I had to grab him by the arm and pull. "Henry!" I said. "What's wrong with you? Stop playing games. It's time to line up." Henry was looking at me like he didn't know who I was. I was relieved when he finally unfolded himself from the chair and moved toward the door.

The rain started to really pour down then. No chance of outside recess. As we were leaving, I turned my head to say to Henry, "Guess we're stuck inside again." And that's when I noticed that Henry had left his sketchbook behind on the chair. I was the very last person in line, so I went to get it for him. By the time I returned, the rest of the class was a little ahead of me, down the hall. As I walked toward them, I glanced at the page Henry had been working on, and it was the strangest thing.

In the center of the page was a squiggle, like a line of cursive handwriting. Except that it didn't form any words I could make sense of. It was too neat to be just a scribble, though. It looked too much like handwriting to be a random design. I couldn't figure it out, and I hate it when I can't figure things out. I could have asked Henry, I suppose, but he had been acting so weird that I was afraid he'd just snatch the sketchbook before I had a chance to solve the riddle.

Back in the classroom, we had silent reading time. We got to sit wherever we wanted; this time I was the one who headed for a corner. I hid Henry's sketchbook behind a big book about Egypt and stared at what Henry had drawn.

Come find me

Was it a foreign language? Was that it? Henry was pretty smart. Maybe the letters didn't look right because it wasn't English. Maybe that was it. But then it came to me, and my hand shot into the air. I had to leave. I asked Biniam for permission to go to the bathroom. Then I bolted down the hallway with Henry's sketchbook clutched to my chest.

The bathroom was empty, so I walked to the sink and held the sketchbook up to the mirror. Instantly the letters reversed themselves and fell into their proper order. The lights flickered; then there it was again:

Come find me

The air around me seemed to grow cold as I stared into the mirror. I knew I was alone, but suddenly it felt like someone was there, like someone had tapped me, gently, on the shoulder.

I spun around. And as I raced out into the hall, dropping the sketchbook, I swear I could hear Edgar behind me. Laughing.

I flew through the classroom door, out of breath and terrified. And everyone there was still reading, lost in their own little worlds. The only one who even looked up was Ms. Biniam.

"Barbara Anne?" she asked. "Are you all right?"

Henry looked over then, and I knew he was listening. I knew he realized, or would soon, that Edgar was at it again.

"I'm okay," I said, but my voice sounded shaky, and I wasn't sure she believed me.

"Do you feel well?" she asked. "Would you like to go see the nurse?"

The nurse! That was a good one. If only someone could just put a bandage on this whole thing and make it go away.

"No," I said. "I just . . . I bumped into someone, and it startled me. I'll be okay as soon as I sit down."

But then I realized that it was still out there, in the hallway, Henry's sketchbook. "I just need a minute to get something from my locker," I told Biniam.

Instead, I walked down the empty hallway and stooped to pick up the sketchbook. When I turned around, I jumped. Henry was standing right behind me. "Henry! Don't do that!"

"Do what?"

"Sneak up on me like that," I said.

"I'm sorry," Henry said. "Are you okay? What happened?"

His voice was kind, and he looked worried. And in that moment, I was so happy to have him back, the real Henry, my Henry, who recognized me and was still my friend, my first real friend. My eyes filled with tears.

Henry hugged me and awkwardly patted my back. "It's okay," he said.

"Hey," I told him, wiping my eyes. "I need to show you something."

And as we walked back, I explained about the sketchbook and the message. All of it.

It was still scary, of course, but not nearly as bad with Henry by my side.

CHAPTER NINE

THE COSTUME PARADE

It's a tradition at Washington Carver to parade around the block in costume on Halloween. Some kids think it's baby-ish, but I still think it's fun. Of course, it would have been more fun if Biniam hadn't forced us to make that huge list of rules that ruined lots of our costumes. I came as a witch, but some kids just gave up completely on being anything scary. You could see it right away as soon as we lined up: football player, ballerina, firefighter, and—I wish I were making this up—Alonzo dressed up as broccoli. Broccoli!

"Very creative," Ms. Biniam told him.

"He's a vegetable," I muttered. "A vegetable. This is pro-paganda!"

"I know," Henry said. "What's next? A giant toothbrush?"

"What are you supposed to be?" Zack asked, looking at Henry's dark pants and white shirt. "A waiter?"

"No!" Henry said. "A vampire!"

"That's why he has the cape," I pointed out.

"I might as well be a waiter," Henry said. "My costume looks pathetic without the makeup."

"What are you?" I asked Zack.

"The Green Weeper," he said. "Just without the sigh because of the weapons thing."

"The Green Weeper?" Henry asked.

"You know," Zack said. "Death."

"That's the Grim Reaper, you idiot," Henry told him.

"And it's a scythe," I added.

"Well, aren't you two just the experts on everything!" Zack said.

"Stop all this fighting!" Renee yelled. "We're supposed to be having FUN." She was scowling at us, her hands on her hips. She was dressed as the Easter bunny.

"Ten," Zack said. "Nine, eight . . ."

We stared at him. "It's for calming down, OKAY?!" he yelled. And then he lowered his voice a bit. "Everyone needs to just settle down."

"Okay, kids," said our room mom. "Time to line up! Single file."

Right. Because nothing says party like being ordered to line up.

"We need to take turns, so we can exit the building in an orderly fashion," the room mom said. Then she pointed to Alonzo. "Broccoli boy, you can be our line leader."

"Broccoli boy!" Zack hooted.

"Yeah," Henry said. "Something tells me that one's gonna stick for a while."

Outside, the wind pushed dry leaves along the sidewalk at our feet. Our parents and grandparents and neighbors lined the edge of the sidewalk and waved at us. "Here they come!" someone yelled. People held up phones to take our pictures.

"Renee!" someone shouted. "Smile!"

Renee turned her head and flashed a smile.

"Are your parents coming?" I asked Zack.

"They have to work," Zack said. Zack's parents are doctors who work long hours and sometimes have to leave right in the middle of dinner or a trip to the zoo because of being "on call," whatever that means.

"Mine too," Henry added.

"Who cares?" Zack said. "We're too old for this anyhow, if you ask me."

"You're just crabby 'cause you can't eat all the candy on account of your braces," Renee told him.

"It's not fair," Zack said. "No popcorn either."

"I see someone!" I said. "My mom's here." She waved at

me. She had Rachel in the stroller. Rachel was dressed up like a pumpkin. She looked so cute! "Hey, Henry," I said. "Look at Rachel's costume. She's a pumpkin."

"Where?" Henry asked. And when I pointed them out, he said, "Oh, I see them now. They're right next to Miss Leary."

"Who?" I asked.

"Constance Leary. The older lady in the wheelchair. She's a friend of Sophie's from church."

She was old, all right. REALLY old. She had dark glasses on and a blanket on her lap.

"Is she blind?" I asked him.

"Almost," he said. "She's got this one weird eye that's like all cloudy."

I stared at the old woman. Something about her bothered me for the rest of the parade. It wasn't the description of her eye—creepy as that was. It was something else, and I couldn't figure it out. Until, finally, I realized that it was her name: Constance Leary.

"We have to stop at my locker," I said to Henry.

"What for? The party's starting. Renee says we get to watch a movie."

"This will only take a second!" I said.

Honestly, all we were missing was a popcorn ball and the start of some cartoon called *Herbie's Halloween*. I needed to get to my locker. I needed to take another look at that year-book from the trunk.

It took some time for me to dig it out. Henry disapproved of the state of my locker.

"Is that greenish thing a sandwich?" he asked.

"Yeah, I should throw that out," I said.

"You think?"

"Henry, please try to focus. Not everybody is a total neat freak like you. Oh, here it is! *Our Golden School Days.*"

We sat down cross-legged on the floor and opened it. This time I wasn't looking for Edgar. There weren't too many pages in the book, so it didn't take long to find her. She looked nothing like the old lady in the wheelchair, of course, but the name was right.

Constance Leary
Nickname: Freckles

"That's strange," Henry said, staring at the old photograph. "What's her picture doing in my attic?"

CHAPTER TEN

TRICK OR TREAT?

Henry and I wanted to trick-or-treat by ourselves, of course. And my mom promised that we could go alone as long as we stayed together and checked in with her in exactly one hour. Renee was thinking of meeting us too, but that might not work. Her dad was still deciding. And Zack, well, we didn't ask Zack. He was going with this big group of obnoxious boys who all played soccer together.

I felt pretty confident about the whole thing. I had a really cute canvas bag (orange to match my black-and-orange witch tights), and I told my mom that I understood that some of the candy would have to go into the freezer. (This would not be a problem, really, because I could always get it back from my grandmother later, piece by piece, or hide a little under my bed.) I was all set.

Henry, however, was not prepared. It wasn't his fault, really. It was Sophie—as usual. She was afraid that if he wore vampire makeup, he would scare little kids. But (a) being scared is the whole point of Halloween. Plus, (b) she clearly underestimates children. Does she really think we are so easily terrified?

Sophie doesn't understand anything about what's scary. She works at the zoo. What does she have to be afraid of? Except maybe getting bitten by a lion, if they ask her to feed one. I'm sure she has training for that. And it seems pretty easy. I've seen trainers go inside the cages. It happens all the time on television.

Anyway, I was prepared to solve Henry's costume problems whether Sophie liked it or not. Inside my canvas Halloween bag was a little fake blood. Just a small tube, not too dried out, from last year. I'd snagged it, when my mom wasn't looking, from the face-paint bin she keeps in the crawl space for when she's in charge of the school carnival.

The plan was perfect except for one thing: Alice.

As soon as my mom and I got to Henry's house, and she saw Alice in costume, she started to gush. "Oh, look, Alice in Wonderland! Are you going along too?"

Henry looked like he was going to be sick, but Alice just put on her sweetest face, smiled at my mom, and said, "If they let me."

Honestly, sometimes she is such a phony.

So of course we were stuck with her. Henry's dad and my mom reviewed all the rules about staying together and how long we had (one hour timed out on Henry's watch) and where we had to meet (the new coffee place, on the corner, down the hill).

"How could you let this happen?" I asked Henry as soon as we got away from my mom.

"Me?" Henry asked. "Your mom is the one who started it."

"Well, your sister is the one who asked."

"Look," Henry said. "Do you want to spend the whole time fighting, or do you want to get some candy?"

He had a point, I suppose. And it probably isn't a good idea to complain too much about a guy's sister. Even if the guy is your best friend.

"I can keep up," Alice said. (I guess she had been listening the whole time.)

And then we were off.

"Oh, wait!" I said as soon as Henry, Alice, and I reached the bottom step at the first house.

"We have to hurry!" Henry told me.

"This will only take a second. I brought you something." I pulled the tube out of my canvas bag. Henry stared at it.

"Come here," I said. Henry was being obstinate, so I pushed his head to one side a little bit, stood on my tiptoes, and went to work.

"What are you doing?" Alice asked.

"Vampire blood."

"Sophie said we can't use that," Alice said.

"Just leave it off," Henry said.

"Henry, it doesn't look right without it," I said. "I've got this."

Then I bent down on one knee and said, "Alice, we're letting you come with us, which is really nice of us, and you're going to keep a little secret about the vampire blood so your brother can have some fun for once in his life. GOT IT?"

"Fine!" Alice said. "You win."

"See?" I told Henry. "Problem solved. I'm very good with children."

"You're scarier than anything else out here," Henry said. But he had a little smile on his face, and there was no hiding it. Henry wanted to see the fake blood, but we had no time and no mirror, so I said, "It looks perfect. Just trust me." And we knocked on the front door.

The first few houses went great. We even got a

regular-sized candy bar at one stop and a whole fistful of candy at another place, where somebody was throwing a party.

"We're lucky," Henry said. "I bet not a single kid in there gets to go trick-or-treating like this."

"Yep. *Too dangerous*," I said.

"As if our parents aren't going to check every piece," Alice said. "And Sophie will probably turn half of it in to the dentist."

"Biniam," Henry and I said at the same time, and then laughed.

"You can make a lot of money giving candy to the dentist. They pay you by the pound!" Alice said as we passed a low shrub. And as soon as the words left her mouth, a dark shape leapt in front of us.

"Give me your candy, kid!"

I jumped about a foot in the air. Alice screamed and dropped her plastic pumpkin.

Henry said, "Put down the axe, Zack. We know it's you."

"You're no fun," Zack said.

Henry collected Alice's fallen candy from the ground and took her by the hand.

"We gotta go, Zack," I said. "We're kind of in a hurry."

"Can I come?" Zack asked.

"I thought you were going with your soccer friends," Henry said.

"He can come if he wants to. It's a free country," Alice announced before Zack could even explain. She was getting to be so sassy.

The four of us had a pretty good system going. Henry led the way and rang the doorbells and always said that his little sister was on her way. If you go in a group, you don't want the oldest kid to show up first because sometimes you get a crabby old person who says, "Aren't you kind of *big* to be trick-or-treating?" You'd think they'd be sympathetic about the whole age thing, but no. First, they complain. Then they toss in something large, like an apple, that smashes all of your stuff.

Anyway, we were almost finished, and we were having fun, Zack or no Zack. I thought maybe I'd tell them a few fun facts about Halloween. "Did you know that Halloween started out as a type of begging? For these things called soul cakes?" I asked.

Zack groaned. "Not now, Barbara Anne."

"We're trying to hurry," Alice said.

"Yeah," Henry said. "We're begging. Begging you not to tell us!"

"Fine!" I said. "Remain ignorant. You're the ones losing out. I already know this stuff."

It was dark out, but I'm pretty sure I saw Alice roll her eyes at me. Alice!

Soon we were back where we'd started, with only a few houses to go before the coffee place. One of them was right across the street from Henry's house. It was old and creepy, with vines twisting up around the porch and no decorations out front. A dim light glowed in an upstairs window, but the whole bottom portion of the house was dark. The place was spooky. Super spooky. Like *Dare you to go up there* spooky.

"Maybe we should skip this one," I said.

"We can't skip this one," Alice said. "It's Miss Leary's house. Sophie will be mad."

"Miss Leary?" I asked Henry. "The old lady from the parade?"

"Yeah," he said.

I pictured her staring at us with her horrible ruined eyeball, dipping her ancient, gnarled fingers into our bags and touching all our candy.

"But her house isn't decorated or anything, Alice," I said. "I don't think she's participating in Halloween."

Zack snorted. "*Participating?* It's not a field trip. Knock on the door, you chicken."

"Why don't you do it?" Alice asked. (Maybe it wasn't entirely bad having her along.)

"Yeah, why don't you go? You're the one carrying a weapon," Henry said.

"That's true," Zack said. "I do look way scarier than any of you."

That's what he said, but he didn't exactly rush up to the door. In fact, he didn't take one step toward the door.

"He's not going to do it," Alice said. "Big talk. No action."

"Listen, Alice in Wonderland," Zack said. "I've got this. Just give me a minute, okay?"

In the dark, it was hard to see his face, but his voice wavered just enough to let us know he was scared. It was horrible to watch, but it wasn't like we were going to stop looking. So I pushed Alice behind me, and we took a few steps back. Then we waited on the sidewalk, eyes glued to Zack. Time slowed.

"Henry, I don't think this is a very good idea after all," Alice said.

"Shhhh!" Henry and I told her, but maybe Alice was right. I mean, who knew who was inside? I mean, I knew who was inside, but who knew who she was? Well, her name. Yes. Constance. But . . .

"Henry—" I started to say, but then he shushed me too. And the three of us watched as Zack rang the bell.

Nothing.

We waited. The door remained shut, but somewhere

another one opened. We could hear it: a long, slow *eeeeeeeek* sort of sound. And that was all it took to terrify us.

I know we should have been braver. There were four of us: Death (in the lead), then a witch, a vampire, and Alice in Wonderland. But we just stood there, mesmerized, as Zack stared at the house. We were waiting to see who—or what—would emerge from that dark, awful place. We held our breath. And then a loud, metallic *CLANG* broke the silence, followed by a heavy thud.

"Run!" Henry shouted.

And we did.

CHAPTER ELEVEN

ARTIFACTS

As soon as Halloween was over, Biniam was straight back to business. I mean, she started piling on the homework. All the teachers were doing it. It was like they had some rule book that told them to be sure we never had fun two days in a row. And Biniam's torture was the worst one of all. We had to write an artifact paper, which is where you take something old, like an object or a photo, and you explain in detail about the time it came from.

Our class was in the library at school. We were supposed to be working on it, but we were having trouble getting started. Biniam even had this box of old junk and photos you could pick from if you wanted, but none of it looked interesting. Mixed in were some random objects like a lightbulb, this weird white hat with a cross stitched into it, and a small wooden box with marbles inside.

"It's not the object that matters so much," Biniam tried to tell us. "Once you choose, you have a mystery to solve, a story to tell. Think of yourself as a detective!"

We kept digging through the box. Then Zack grabbed the hat and put it on his head. Once it was unfolded, we could see that it hung down in back, like a veil.

"Here comes the bride," Henry said.

Zack flung that thing off his head so fast you would have thought it was on fire. It was too late, of course. Kids were already starting to laugh, and Zack suddenly looked furious. "If you weren't my friend!" he yelled at Henry. Zack's face was bright red.

"Zack," said Ms. Biniam. "Take a breath."

Everything stopped for a minute then, and the whole class watched to see if Zack was going to explode. But Biniam walked over to him and quietly suggested that he go get a drink of water. After he left, she launched into an immediate lecture on taking the project more seriously.

It made me feel sort of guilty, so I picked up the cap Zack left behind and looked at it. "Ms. Biniam," I asked. "Did this belong to a nurse?"

"It did, Barbara Anne."

"Well, I get the lightbulb," Renee told Ms. Biniam.

"Bright idea," Alonzo said. Nobody laughed. People were staring. But Alonzo just couldn't leave it alone. "Bright idea? Get it?"

"This is the worst project ever," Henry whispered. "What am I supposed to use? There's nothing left to pick."

"You can have this if you want," Alonzo said, and he handed the wooden box with the marbles to Henry.

"I don't want that; it's a silly kids' game," Henry said. "Maybe my mom will have an idea the next time I talk to her. Or maybe I can call Uncle Marty. I don't know what to choose. I guess I'm just tired."

But it seemed like more than that. I was studying his face, and it seemed like much more. And eventually Henry told me—about the dream he had the night before.

"I woke up," Henry said. "Or, I thought I woke up. And there was this smell in the room. And I felt someone's hand on my forehead. Then when my eyes adjusted to the dark, I could see it was a woman, sitting on the edge of my bed, staring at me. I don't know why, but she had this mask on her face."

"Like a Halloween mask?" I asked.

"No. Like the kind a doctor wears."

"A surgical mask?"

"Yeah," Henry said. "I guess so. It was so strange. It seemed so . . . real."

"Wow," I said, "so there's two of them! Two ghosts. Well, some places are like that, Henry. I saw this show once about a haunted hotel, and—"

"My house is not a haunted hotel, Barbara Anne!"

Biniam looked over at us, and I was afraid she might start listening, so I whispered. "At least tell me this. What was the smell?"

"Lilacs," Henry answered. "It smelled like lilacs."

We didn't get anything done after that. I put the nurse hat back, Henry spent his time doodling in his sketchbook, and I was extremely busy watching the clock. I was going to ask Biniam what time our class was over, but I had noticed that teachers get all insulted whenever somebody brings it up. Anyway, gym was next—rope climbing—and I didn't really want to think about that either.

"Too bad we can't use the stuff from the trunk," I said.

"Sure," Henry said. "Great idea. 'Found this in my house, which, by the way, is haunted.'"

"You'd probably get an A. It's way more interesting than a lightbulb."

Henry ignored me.

"I'm just saying . . ."

The clock ticked. I'd never noticed before how loud it was. Then I raised my hand—to ask for a drink of water. But of course I wasn't really thirsty. I was going to get the only artifacts that really interested me. The ones from the trunk.

Henry was not too happy when he saw the pile of stuff in my hands.

"So, what?" Henry asked. "You just walk around the hall-way carrying that stuff now? You don't even *try* to hide it?"

"If you act like it's not a big deal, nobody will know it's a big deal."

"You're gonna end up in jail someday," Henry said. "And I'm not going to visit you."

Henry had a lot more to say. Sometimes he gets more talkative when he's mad. Either that or he stops speaking completely. It can go either way. I just let him finish, but I wasn't really listening closely.

". . . you think nobody knows what you're doing, but eventually someone's going to ask!" He was staring at me. "Are you *wearing* the locket?" he asked.

I shrugged. "It looks good on me." And, really, nobody could argue with that.

Now, here's the weird part. Henry and I were sitting off by ourselves, at a table far away from the windows. But during Henry's big lecture about the need for secrecy, we suddenly felt a gust of air or wind. It was so strong that it pushed the scrapbook/yearbook right off the table, smack onto the floor. It popped open, and an old, yellowish piece of paper fell out—a newspaper article.

Henry and I looked at each other, too surprised to say anything. Then I raced to grab the article. "What does it say?" Henry asked. He was reading over my shoulder.

WASHINGTON STATE, May 21, 1925
Memorial Day Poppy Sale

A special Memorial Day service will be celebrated this year at the Legion Post on Main Street. In preparation, the poppy sale will begin a few days before. Everyone will want to have a poppy to wear to the ceremony in remembrance of Flanders fields.

After the flag ceremony, we will take flowers to the Mountain View Cemetery to decorate the old soldiers' graves.

"Think it has anything to do with Edgar?" I asked.

"I don't know," Henry said. "But stick it back in the book before anyone sees it."

So I opened the book to slip the article back inside, and that's when I saw it. The photo. He was older, but it still looked like him. I stared at his face.

"What?" Henry asked.

"This guy in the yearbook," I said, pointing. "Phillip Winterson. He looks like the kid in the trunk photo. The one who's standing in front of a piano with his music teacher."

"You're right," Henry said. "He does."

"Henry, do you think this guy could be Edgar's older brother?"

"Maybe," Henry said. "It's hard to say."

"I mean, why else would his picture be in your house? Henry, you haven't ever . . . seen him, have you?"

"What? Like, floating around my room? No, Barbara Anne. I haven't. And I don't want to either. Two ghosts are more than enough."

"Wait!" I said. "Phillip Winterson? That's P. Winterson. The yearbook belongs to him. He has to be Edgar's brother. Bring the photo to school tomorrow. So we can compare. Then we'll know a hundred percent for sure."

Then the bell rang, and we headed off to gym.

I was so busy running errands after school with my mom that I almost forgot about the article. But when we got home, I took it out again and reread it.

"Dinner's in twenty minutes!" my mom shouted.

But I didn't wait that long to join my parents. I had too many questions. My parents were in the kitchen, cooking.

When I walked in, Rachel was in her high chair, flinging blueberries all over the floor.

"What are Flanders fields?" I asked.

"World War One," my dad said. "They're famous battlefields in Belgium." Then he turned to my mom and asked, "There's a poem too, right?"

"Yeah," she said. "'In Flanders fields the poppies blow / Between the crosses, row on row.'"

"Why?" my dad asked.

"Nothing," I said. "School project."

"World War One?" my dad asked my mom. "Aren't they a little young for that?"

"Your baby's growing up," my mom said.

And I went back to my room. I kept trying to figure out what it all meant, what it had to do with Edgar. All I really had, though, were a few clues that weren't exactly adding up. So I took out a sheet of paper and tried to make notes.

1925 = World War 1

Then I crossed that out. They were remembering the war in 1925, so it must have started earlier. I went to my dad's office to look up the dates on the computer.

July 28, 1914, to November 11, 1918.

Then I looked up "Flanders fields," and that's when I

found out how famous the poem is. It was written by this Canadian guy named John McCrae. And it's basically a poem written by ghosts. The whole thing is like a story told by dead guys from World War I. Well, I mean, McCrae wrote it, so I guess he was just saying what the dead guys would have said. He looked like a nice man, from the picture. He wasn't smiling or anything, of course, but his face looked kind.

My parents were yelling from the kitchen then—that it was time for dinner. So I didn't get much further. I started to skim. But I did find out this: John McCrae wasn't just a poet. He was a soldier and a doctor too. He worked in the medical corps in France. And he died of pneumonia.

The next day, at recess, Henry and I compared the photos, the large one of the boy and older man in front of the piano, and the yearbook photo of Phillip Winterson. The yearbook photo did look like a slightly older version of the same boy. Whoever he was, he'd gone to school with Constance Leary. Someday, if we were brave enough to ask, she might be able to identify him.

"Phillip probably is Edgar's brother, or his friend," Henry said. "That makes sense. But who do you think Thomas was?"

"Thomas?"

"Yeah," Henry said. "The letter. It's addressed to Thomas."

"I don't understand the letter at all," I admitted. "The same stuff keeps coming up, though. France and the army and pneumonia."

Three clues.

Later that night, I went into my dad's office again and I typed in "France army pneumonia." And this popped up.

The U.S. Military and the Influenza Pandemic of 1918–1919

I clicked on the black-and-white photo above the first entry, and there they were, men in long gowns and masks and women in white hats with crosses, like the one in Ms. Biniam's artifact box. They were staring back at me like they'd been waiting for me to find them. It took me a second to realize they were doctors and nurses, that the long, ghostly white shapes behind them were just sheets suspended around the metal beds of patients with pneumonia.

CHAPTER TWELVE

SNAPSHOTS

Henry and I sat together at lunch every day now, whether we were required to or not. Some days we talked the whole time. Some days Henry read his comic book and ignored everyone—even though I told him it was rude to read at the table. What he didn't usually do was sit there saying nothing, staring off into space, and then coughing into his elbow.

"You feeling okay, Henry?"

"What?"

"Earth to Henry," I said.

Even Rodney laughed at him, but that didn't seem to register with Henry either. "Are you almost finished eating?" he asked. "I need to ask you something."

"Ask away," I said, still chewing on my sandwich.

"Not here," he said. And he looked serious, so serious that I tossed the last of my lunch in the garbage and headed out to the playground.

"No one ever tells me anything!" Rodney yelled as we left him behind.

As soon as we were out the door, Henry said, "I found something weird. This morning, at the foot of my bed, by the window."

"What?" I asked.

I knew that was Edgar's spot—one of his spots, anyway. So I expected something stranger than what Henry said next.

"Circles," he told me.

"Circles?"

He stopped walking then and took out his sketchbook. "Yeah," he said. "Circles. Like this. Drawn on the floor in chalk. What do you think it means?" he asked.

"I don't know," I said. I stared at his drawing—a circle, within a circle, within a circle—each one larger, the way water ripples outward when you drop a stone in a lake.

"I mean, I know it has to be him. Edgar. But why? What does he want?" Henry asked.

"Maybe he's trying to hypnotize you somehow," I said.

"What?"

"You know, like put you into some sort of a trance."

"I know what 'hypnotize' means, Barbara Anne!"

"Well, they use circles for that, you know. Especially spinning ones."

"Never mind," Henry said. "I'm sorry I asked."

It was ungrateful of him, really. Unreasonable. I was trying my best to understand what it all meant, and Henry wasn't giving me any credit at all. I might have stopped speaking to him, except that I felt kind of bad that he didn't feel well. Also, I had something I wanted to ask him. I kept thinking about those pictures, the ones of the masked doctors that I'd seen on my father's computer. No matter what I did, I couldn't seem to forget them—their look-right-through-you stares and their folded arms. The nurses wore white caps just like the one in Ms. Biniam's artifact box. I know it sounds crazy, but it felt like they wanted something from me, like they *expected* it. So I had to keep going.

First, I had to convince Henry that we needed to take another look at both photos from the trunk. There was the one with Edgar and the others standing on the porch of Henry's house, and the second one, which didn't even have Edgar in it, of the tall boy and the older man in front of a piano.

"You know what I think?" I asked Henry as we walked home together.

"Is there any way you won't tell me?" Henry asked.

"Good point," I said. "I think we need a magnifying glass. You know, so we can really inspect the photos."

"In case there's a ghost in the background?" Henry asked.

"Exactly!" I said.

Henry was being a sarcastic brat, but I knew I could convince him because I'd been doing some reading, and I had a mountain of evidence. Not to brag.

Henry sighed a great big *Here it comes* sort of sigh, but I said, "Just listen." And then I told him all about Arthur Conan Doyle and the Crewe Circle and all this other cool stuff I'd been reading about. Obviously, Arthur Conan Doyle is famous for creating Sherlock Holmes, but he also wrote this unusual book that is partly about World War I and partly a collection of poetry and partly a bunch of photographs. It's the photographs that are the most interesting because they have ghosts in them.

"So what are you saying, Barbara Anne? It's like a ghost yearbook?"

"No," I said. "Say you were dead and I was still alive and—"

"How come I have to be the dead one?"

"It doesn't matter who the dead one is!" I said. "Okay, I'll be the dead one. So, after I die, you go to this photography studio run by the Crewe Circle to get your picture taken. And it's just you posing for the picture, but then, when you get it back, I'm there in the background. Like, a faint ghostly image of me."

"You photobomb my portrait?" Henry asked.

"Yeah. Sort of."

"You come back from the afterlife to wreck my picture?" Henry asked. "To distract from me and get all the attention for yourself?"

"No!" I said. "It doesn't ruin the picture. It makes it more interesting, more special. The background image was always somebody they knew, like a friend or a relative, somebody who had died that they missed. And they were glad to know the person was still there somehow."

"Really?" Henry asked. He didn't seem convinced.

"Or," I said, "sometimes they found the person's handwriting on the picture. And that was part of how they proved that the ghostly background person really was their dead friend."

"What?"

"Because the handwriting matched. Like, say you had a note from me. From before I died, obviously. And then you see a message in the background of your portrait. And it's in my handwriting. But how can it be? Because now I'm dead. And then you take the photo and the old note, and you look at them, and they match. Perfectly. So it's like I'm still talking to you even though I'm dead."

"Great," Henry said. "I'll look forward to that."

"So that's why we need the magnifying glass!" I told him.

"To check for mail from dead guys?"

"Exactly."

Henry didn't need to say anything else. I could tell from the look on his face that he thought the whole thing was a big fat fake. But he went into this endless explanation anyway, about how they must have done something to the negatives to play a trick on everyone. His dad is really interested in photography, so Henry gave me this huge, boring lecture about film and negatives and how light works.

"You're missing the point," I said. "These Coven Circle people are the ones who made the photos a long time ago in England. And they said the negatives never left the photographer's hands."

"Really?" Henry asked, in a way that made it clear that he did not, even for ten seconds, believe me.

"Yes," I said.

"I thought you said it was Crewe Circle, which makes more sense, since a coven is a witch thing, not a ghost thing. You know that, right?"

I didn't know that. But I certainly did not need Henry to tell me. "So what's your point?" I asked.

"My point," Henry said, "is I think you've got your facts wrong."

We were standing in front of Henry's house by then. It's sort of embarrassing to admit this, but I got so involved in our conversation that I just never turned when we came to my street.

"Want to come in and ask my dad?" Henry said.

"Yeah," I said, because I am not one to back down from a dare, which is clearly what this was. Even so, I had a sinking feeling that Henry would be gloating soon, and I was not looking forward to his *I'm right again* happy dance. Lucky for me, his dad had something to say, and it had nothing to do with photography or ghosts. He hit us with it as soon as we got through the front door.

"Your mom wants you to go over and rake Miss Leary's leaves," his dad said.

"My mom's not even in the country," Henry said. "Barbara Anne's here, and Sophie said I could have her over."

Now, this was both an outright lie and an unusually sassy answer coming from Henry. To understand it, you really have to know these things:

1. His mom was still in England studying English.
2. Henry hates it when his dad calls Sophie his mom, because she is only his stepmom.
3. Henry was trying to get out of his chores, as usual, by using me as an excuse.
4. I hate when he does that.

I guess number four, technically, is about me and not about Henry, but I count too, right?

"It won't take long," Henry's dad said. "The two of you can do it together. You and, uh, what's your name, kid?"

I smiled. Every time I'm over there, Henry's dad does this same bad joke about how he's forgotten my name. It's sort of stupid but sort of sweet.

"Let's go," Henry said. He tossed down his books on the stairs, and we left.

That's the thing about Henry. I love him, but sometimes he gives up so easily.

"Have fun!" Henry's dad called from the couch.

I guess I was so focused on all the bickering that it hadn't really sunk in. Where Henry and I were going. Miss Leary's house. Halloween house. The one we had all run from screaming just a few nights before. When Henry saw the look on my face, he said, "It's okay. Sophie knows her. She goes to our church."

I must have looked as unconvinced as I felt, because he said, "She's harmless, Barbara Anne. You saw her at the costume parade. Does she look like she has the strength to hurt anybody?"

"I couldn't see anything," I said. "She was all covered up with a blanket and dark glasses."

"She's an old lady! She's got a problem with her eye."

"Oh, yeah," I said. "Thanks for reminding me. I can't wait to see that!"

"You should go home," Henry said. "If you're going to act like a baby, go home."

Well, that did it. Nobody was going to tell me when I had to leave. Except maybe my mom, or my dad, or my grandmother, or Sophie. But not a kid! So I helped Henry rake the lawn. Miss Leary's helper lady, the one who pushes her wheelchair, brought us two rakes from the garage and a couple of giant garbage bags. The leaves were sort of wet and slimy, and it was hard work getting them all into two big piles.

"I wish they were dry," Henry said. "We could jump in them. My mom and Alice and I used to do that at the old house."

"You miss it, don't you?" I asked.

"Yeah," he said. But we both knew he was talking more about his mom than the house. I knew he got to talk to her on the phone sometimes, but I also knew that he must miss her a lot. And I didn't know what to say to him about that. So I tried to distract him by throwing a handful of leaves at him.

"That's disgusting," Henry said. "It's not snow, Barbara Anne!"

But I'd made him smile, and that was a good thing. And

it helped me forget, for a minute, where we were, and how dark it was starting to get.

When the raking was finished, the debate began, between me and Henry. Because he started up the stairs to knock on the door.

"What are you doing?" I asked him. "We finished. We get to go now."

"I'm letting them know," Henry said.

"When they look out the window and see the big garbage bags instead of random leaves, they'll know," I said.

"What are you so afraid of?" Henry asked. "What do you think is in there, anyway?"

I didn't know, but I had some guesses, and vampire bats were at the top of the list.

"Have you ever been in there before?" I asked him. I was working pretty hard to make sure my voice didn't shake.

"No," Henry said, and he just kept going, closer and closer, toward the front door. Then he marched up the steps, so I had no choice. I ran after him and grabbed him by the waist and started to tug. Henry fell, and this is why we ended up in a heap on Miss Leary's doorstep when she answered the bell.

I don't really know what I pictured was behind the door of that house before I went there that day. But what I found surprised me. The house wasn't dark and creepy inside; no bats, not a cobweb in sight. And yet, what happened there was more frightening than anything I could have imagined that Halloween night. It started with a game of checkers, which, I know, sounds harmless. Unless you know what happened next.

Constance Leary asked us in and took us to the living room, which seemed almost like a library. I was looking at all the books while Henry was trying to tell Constance— Miss Leary, I guess I should say—that we didn't need any money for raking the lawn. Not that he'd actually stopped to ask me if I thought we should get paid. He just turned it down.

"Oh, no," he said. "We were glad to do it."

Well, now he was just flat-out fibbing. Who is ever glad to be standing in the cold stuffing wet, smelly leaves into a trash bag? I had gym shoes on, thin ones, and my feet were all wet! And Henry had been coughing so much I was kind of worried about him.

But I didn't care if we got paid; I was just happy that her living room looked normal. Also, I was busy not looking at Miss Leary's face when she talked. You know—because of the whole eye thing. Inside, she didn't wear the dark glasses, so it was easier to see her face, her eyes. And one of them had this filmy, swirly pattern like a marble (even though your eye would be more like a hard-boiled egg, I guess). It was sort of fascinating but mostly gross to think about, and hard to look at too, so I turned toward the bookcases.

They lined the whole wall of the room. There was even another one just outside, in the hallway. I stepped out there to look at it. And that's when the first weird thing happened. I was standing near the foot of a staircase, my head tilted, reading titles, when I heard a funny noise. I turned to look and saw a real marble bouncing down the wooden steps. It landed at my feet, and I picked it up. I was holding it, studying its blue and white twists, when it happened again. Two more. A green-and-yellow one—and another, larger and solid white. I picked them up and put them in my pocket.

Then I looked toward the living room, to see if I could say something to Miss Leary, but she and Henry were still talking. So instead, I went up the stairs. To see who was throwing the marbles. The stairs were creaky, and the hallway above was dark. Halfway up, I was already regretting my choice, but I had to know who was there.

"Hello?" I called out.

No answer. And the hallway, when I got there, was empty. Every room was dark. I walked back down the stairs sideways. I was not about to turn my back on whoever or whatever was up there.

When I got back to the living room, things turned even weirder. As I walked toward Miss Leary, I heard her say to Henry, "How about a game of checkers, Edgar?"

I stopped and stared at the two of them. Henry didn't even seem to have noticed the name she had just used. Didn't he hear her? What was going on here? I watched as the two of them set the board up together. They seemed to have forgotten all about me. It was like I was standing there all alone now in that cold, drafty room, and I had no idea what to do.

"It's been so long since we played," Constance said next. "Would you like to go first?"

"I always go first!" Henry said.

Everything about him had gotten strange. The way his voice sounded, the too-straight way he was sitting on the chair. Especially the way he was talking to her—as if . . . well, as if he were talking to me. As if they were friends. I couldn't figure it out, but it made me shiver.

"Henry," I said. "It's getting late. We need to go!"

And then he looked at me, *stared* at me. But it was like he didn't have any idea who I was, like Henry had never even seen me before in his life.

CHAPTER THIRTEEN

THE SNOWSTORM

Winter was coming. The resorts had opened early, and some people were already going skiing on the weekends. The rest of us, though, didn't have a prayer of seeing snow. Not in the city. At least, that's what I thought, until one night when I was getting ready for bed, and I heard my dad say, "Looks like it's starting to snow." I ran out of the bathroom with my toothbrush hanging from my mouth to see for myself.

"Barbara Anne!" my mother yelled. But I ignored her and ran to the window to stand next to my dad and study the precipitation.

"What do you think, Bitsy?" he asked.

I was so excited I was willing to overlook his use of

that horrible, babyish nickname. "Snow!" I said. "Definitely snow!"

It was hard to sleep that night. I had argued that I should be able to stay up for a little while longer to see if it was the real deal. You know, sticking snow. But my mom wasn't having any of it. "Whatever it is, it will be there in the morning," she said.

Now, if you've ever lived in Seattle, you know this is clearly not true. Measurable snow inside the city limits is a pretty big event—like a run-outside-right-away-and-roll-a-snowball situation. I think my dad would have caved, but my mom looked at him and said, "United front!" In case you don't know, that's a grown-ups-against-the-kids battle cry. It was over. I was sent to bed.

But in the morning, it was still there—a beautiful blanket of it that closed down school and everything. Yippee! My mom put Rachel in her snowsuit and pulled her around our yard on a little sled while I built a snowman. Then, later, while my mom was making tomato soup for lunch, Henry called and asked if I could meet him down by the lake.

"I don't know," my mom said. "You need lunch, and Rachel needs a nap. I don't think I'd have time to take you."

"I'll eat lunch. And you don't have to take me. I can walk over by myself."

"It's a little far," she said. And I had to pull the super-sad face that usually only works on my dad—or my grandmother if she's in a really good mood.

My mom sighed. "Okay," she said. "You win. But bundle up."

She made me wear so many layers that I was doing this stiff-legged Frankenstein walk all the way to the park. But as soon as I spotted Henry near the playground, I stopped caring. Henry waved, and when I reached him, he told me that Zack and Renee were coming too.

"Since when are you and Zack friends?" I asked him.

Henry shrugged. "He's not so bad," he said. "And Renee didn't get to go with us on Halloween, so I just thought—"

"Yeah," I said. "Good idea."

The world was so perfect covered in snow that I didn't even mind if Henry and I didn't have it all to ourselves.

At first, the four of us had so much fun that we lost all track of time. Zack was landing snowballs with deadly accuracy. They kept hitting right at my collar, slipping down my back, and making me scream. We were cold, wet, and happy, but the light was beginning to fade.

"We should go," Renee said finally. "It's getting late."

"Afraid of the dark?" Zack asked.

"Well," she said. "Stuff has happened here, you know. Once there was even a murder."

"I've heard about that," I said. "You can see her—the ghost girl—walking around the lake."

"No," Renee said. "You have to walk out toward the point to see her."

"Why?" I asked.

"That's her spot," Renee said. "Ghosts have a spot. They don't just show up anywhere."

"So let's go out there," Zack said.

"I think it's time to get going," Henry said.

He had a point. It was getting dark, and a layer of mist stretched across the lake. But Zack was not convinced.

"Too scared?" Zack asked Henry. And for a minute, I could see a trace of the bully he had almost completely stopped being.

"Henry's right," Renee said. "I want to go too."

"Not until we see the ghost!" Zack said. And then he started making all these low moaning noises that, to me, just sounded like he had a stomachache, but Renee was all creeped out.

"Stop it, Zack!" she yelled. "Maybe you think it's just one big game, but I don't. What's the matter with you, anyway? Didn't you ever know anyone who died?"

Renee ran away from us then—toward a bench, where

she stopped and sat. We watched as she drew her knees up to her chest, folded her face into them, and began to sob.

"Oh, shoot!" Zack said. "I forgot."

"Forgot about what?" I asked.

"About her mom," Zack said. And he ran over to Renee.

Henry and I stared at each other. This was news to us. But then, Zack and Renee had both gone to the same school when they were younger, before they changed the districts. Maybe he knew a lot about Renee that we hadn't discovered yet.

"Follow them," Henry said. And so we ran to the bench, where the three of us stood in a circle around Renee. I offered her a Kleenex.

"Are you going to be okay?" Henry asked her.

"I'm freezing," she said. "I want to go home."

None of us could blame her. Zack and Henry and I lived close enough to walk, but Renee was supposed to call her dad. She started crying all over again when she saw there was no charge left on her phone. I would have helped her, of course, but I don't have a cell phone yet. And I really should have one by now. I know third graders who have them. *Third graders!* Anyway, we had to find a phone for Renee. So that's why we went there—to Henry's house. It was just so Renee would calm down. So she could call her dad for a ride.

When the four of us got to Henry's, everybody was out. This would have been great news except that Henry couldn't find his keys. He was afraid they had dropped out of his pocket—somewhere in the park—and were gone for good now. I suggested that we should keep walking to my house, but Zack didn't want to give up on going inside. Maybe all that talk of ghosts had put him in the mood to see one. The rest of us, though, were less enthusiastic. I thought it was a terrible idea, mostly because if I'm going to do something stupid, I'd rather be following my own plan. At least that way, it's easier to answer the "What were you thinking?" question that always comes later.

"I might have a paper clip," Renee said. She was searching her pockets. "Does anybody know how to pick a lock?"

"With a paper clip?" I asked. "The only lock that's going to work on is one of those tiny ones on the front of a diary. Not that I have any experience with that."

And I don't. Except for reading a short and boring section of my cousin Monica's diary, which was her fault, really, because it wouldn't have happened if she had paid attention to me instead of talking on the phone to her boyfriend while painting her toenails.

"Nope," Renee announced. "All I've got is hand sanitizer. Tangerine."

"Good to know," I said. "Where is Henry?"

He had moved away from us, to the garage, and was

running his hand along the window ledge. "I think Sophie taped an extra key here," he said.

"Oh," said Renee. "Wait. I've got a mini flashlight too." She aimed it toward Henry, and some of the light fell through the window onto cobwebs and metal gardening tools that looked like some kind of ancient torture equipment. I was wishing we'd just gone to my house, knocked the snow off our boots, and had a snack. But it was too late now.

"I've found it," Henry said.

When we got inside, we were still creeping along in dim light because Henry was afraid his parents might come home and "catch" us there.

"Henry," I said. "You aren't doing anything wrong. You live here, remember?"

"I'm not allowed to have friends over when nobody's home," Henry told me. "And you, of all people, should know why."

Honestly, one bloody accident and a tiny bit of property damage, and Sophie holds a grudge forever. Anyway, Henry only let us turn on one tiny light on the hall table, so it wouldn't be obvious that we were there.

"Where's your phone?" Renee asked. But before Henry could even answer, Zack had a question of his own. "So, where do you see your ghost?" he wanted to know.

It was too dark to see him clearly, but I could feel Henry glaring at me.

"The first time?" he asked. "He was right there where you're standing."

"Oh," said Zack. Out of words. Just like that.

"But usually," Henry said, "he's upstairs in my room."

Then Henry took Renee to the kitchen, so she could call her dad. Zack and I just stood there dripping in the front hall, not saying much, until the two of them got back. The house was way too dark, and that made it seem later, somehow, than it really was. And why is it that your hearing improves in the dark? You notice every tick and creak, and none of them sound like anything you've heard before.

When Henry and Renee got back, Renee walked right up to Zack and handed him her tiny flashlight.

"What's this for?" Zack asked.

"I thought you'd need it," she said. "To lead everybody up to Henry's room. Since you're so excited to go ghost hunting and everything."

Now, this was a bit of a surprise. Renee didn't usually stand up to Zack. Worse, lately I'd thought she might have some stupid crush on him—because of the way she laughed at all his boring jokes and gave him all these moony-eyed looks.

"Henry never said we could go up," Zack said. "We're not even supposed to be here, right, Henry?"

"I don't care if you go up," Henry said. And just like that, both of them had turned on him.

"Well, do you think he's up there now?" Zack asked.

"He's usually there late at night. Sometimes at the foot of my bed," Henry said. "But you really never know when he'll show up."

"See?" Renee said. "Worth a try."

"*You* want to go up there?" Zack asked.

"Oh, no," Renee said. "I have to wait down here. My dad's coming to get me."

"But we can't wait to hear all about it," I said.

"You're not going either?" Zack asked me. "Oh, I see how it is. The *girls* are too afraid to go up there."

"No, we're not!" I said. "Are we, Renee?"

"Fine!" she said.

And so we all started up the stairs together.

I had been in Henry's house a thousand times; there really was no reason for me to feel so petrified. But as all four of us followed that thin line of light, it felt like we were going into some strange cave, some unexplored space where we definitely didn't belong.

"What's it look like, this ghost?" Zack wanted to know.

"He's not an 'it,'" I said. "He's a boy. Named Edgar."

We stepped through the doorway just as I said Edgar's name. Maybe it was my imagination, but Henry's room seemed colder and darker than the rest of the house. There was this strange noise too, like someone crinkling paper, and a weird, glowing light near Henry's bed.

"What's that?" Renee asked.

"It's just the radio," Henry said. "My dad gave it to me to help me fall asleep. I must have forgotten to turn it off."

I know it sounds ridiculous now, but everyone froze. We just stared at the glowing yellow square on the front of the radio. It seemed . . . *alive*. And then something shifted. I thought I heard wind at first, but then, slowly, it began to seem more like a whisper that almost, but not quite, made sense. "Wind," I thought I heard, and then "stone"?

Henry moved toward it, but before he could reach the radio, it started blasting out music—classical piano. I recognized the melody immediately because it was the same one Henry and I had heard in the music room the night of the school play.

"Turn it off!" I yelled at Henry.

"I'm trying!" he said.

Then the music stopped. And in its place, there was laughter.

That's when Renee screamed. Then the music returned, but it was just four notes now. *Dum-da-duh-dum.* Over and over until Henry was finally able to pull the cord from the wall, and the thing went quiet.

Downstairs, the four of us sat in stunned silence, waiting for Renee's father to show up.

"He can take you guys home," she said. "It's too cold to walk. Too dark."

I took Renee up on her offer right away. Who wouldn't? Henry just stared at us like the traitors that we were as we planned our escape. And Zack. He did the strangest thing of all. He started to hum. It took me a minute, but then I realized that he was humming those same four notes that had been coming out of the radio.

"Quit it!" I yelled at him. "You don't need to try to scare us anymore. We're already petrified."

"I'm trying to figure something out," Zack said. "Oh, man."

"What?" I asked.

"Those notes. Those four notes? Dum-da-duh-dum. D–E–A–D."

"Stop it!" Renee said.

"What's that supposed to mean?" Henry asked.

"Those are the names of the notes. I'm sure of it. My dad's been teaching me guitar."

"So?" Renee said. "That doesn't mean anything."

"Yes, it does," I said. "It's Edgar's way of saying 'boo.'"

After that, I wanted to get home so badly that all I could do was stand there in the hallway in my coat, ready to go. That's how I know for sure what happened next.

I saw the handle turn first. Before the gust of wind. Before the door blew open with a bang and sent snowflakes swirling in.

Henry and I struggled to push it shut. And then there was one last thing—before the door closed completely. I looked across at Miss Leary's house, at the white snow that lay across her walkway, glittering in the porch light. And I watched for a moment as they formed—footprints—one at a time, out of nowhere, heading straight for Miss Leary's.

I didn't wonder until much later why the light was even on, or who she could have been expecting to come to her through the darkness on such a cold and snowy night.

CHAPTER FOURTEEN

THE JOURNAL

Visiting Henry's house the day of the snowstorm scared me more than I'd like to admit. And I felt sort of guilty for running out of there the second Renee's dad showed up in the driveway. I mean, I didn't even wait for Renee. I just ran to the car, pulled the door open, and said, "Hi, Mr. Garcia, I'm Renee's friend Barbara Anne, and I would be really grateful if you could give me a ride home." I believe in self-sufficiency; I really do. But you have to know your limitations too. And that's why I finally decided to get some grown-up help finding out about Edgar.

I showed up at Henry's house one Saturday and rang the bell. "Grab your stuff," I said to him as soon as he answered the door. "We have an appointment."

"An appointment?" he asked.

And I realized then that, from his point of view, it might sound like I was trying to take him to the dentist, so I said, "More like a field trip. Think of it as a field trip."

"I was gonna play some chess with my dad," Henry said.

"Henry!" I said (and I'll admit my voice was a little whiny). "Don't be so boring."

"And I have a cold, Barbara Anne."

I hesitated then because Henry did look a little pale. And ever since the bronchitis, he'd had this inhaler he had to use sometimes. But still, this was urgent. I couldn't let him off the hook. "Oh, come on, Henry," I said. "It's important."

"Why?" Henry asked.

"It's a surprise."

Henry looked uncertain for a minute, but then he went to the top of the basement steps to yell to his dad. His dad does environmental testing—like checking how polluted the air or water is—and he has this whole basement workshop with cool-looking gauges and meters and other stuff that we are not supposed to touch. It seemed like he was ignoring Henry, but eventually he came up the stairs.

"You sure you feel okay?" he wanted to know once Henry had a chance to ask for permission. But he gave in pretty easy. We were just lucky that Sophie was grocery shopping and Alice was at her dance lesson.

"Here," he said as we headed out the door. He handed Henry a scarf. "But when you get back, you need to clean up that mess in your room. I didn't know kids still played marbles. That was old-school even in my day."

"Marbles?" Henry asked.

"Yeah," his dad said. "I assumed that's why you drew all those circles on your bedroom floor."

Henry and I exchanged a look. And while we walked toward the bus stop, I told Henry about the marbles rolling down the stairs at Miss Leary's house.

"Weird," Henry said. "How come you never told me before?"

"I would have," I said. "But you and Miss Leary were busy. Playing checkers."

"Checkers?" Henry asked.

"Yeah," I said. "Don't you remember?"

"No," Henry said. And he looked upset.

"You just forgot, Henry. It's not a big deal," I said. I didn't want to tell him more, didn't want to find out if he remembered Miss Leary calling him Edgar.

"Barbara Anne, do you think my dad is right?" Henry asked. "Do you think the circles are just a game? I wipe them away, and they keep coming back."

"I don't know," I said.

Later, while we were riding on the bus, Henry turned to me with a strange look on his face. "What?" I asked.

"My dream," Henry said. "That's the first thing he ever said to me. 'Play with me!'"

Henry and I were quiet for a while, but as the bus got closer to downtown, he kept asking me where we were going. He pestered me like a fly at a picnic, but I wouldn't tell him. I was using the same technique my mom does when I have to get new school shoes: don't say anything until you're almost there, and all opportunity for escape is past. Besides, I was afraid that if I announced our destination, Henry would feel hugely disappointed. I'd made it sound like such a top-secret mission that he was probably picturing the two of us taking an elevator to a strange old building and knocking out a coded message on some mysterious door.

Once we got off the bus and it became clear where we were headed, Henry stopped walking entirely and stared at me.

"The library?" he asked. "Really? That's the big emergency?"

"Keep an open mind, Henry," I said.

I was afraid Henry might stop following me, so I tried not to talk and instead just walked as fast as I could into the library and up the escalator. When we arrived at the counter marked REFERENCE, the man behind it smiled at me and tilted his wrist to look at his watch.

"You must be Barbara Anne," he said. "You're right on time."

Then he spotted Henry. "Henry Davis!" he said. "What are you doing here?"

"You know Mr. Corrigan?" I asked, amazed.

"Mr. Corrigan!" Henry laughed. "That's Uncle Marty."

"Henry is my honorary nephew," Mr. Corrigan said. "His mother and I have known each other for years. I was her history teacher, way back in the day. How is your mom, Henry?"

"She's fine," Henry said. "I'll tell her you said hello when she calls on Sunday."

"Do that!" Uncle Marty said. He smiled at Henry.

I liked Uncle Marty already. He looked a little older than our parents but not as old as my grandmother, somewhere in between, and everything about him was gray: his hair, his sweater, the frames of his glasses, even his eyes.

"So, what are we doing here?" Henry asked, looking from Uncle Marty to me. "What's this all about?

"Well, it's pretty simple, really," Uncle Marty said. "Your girlfriend asked me—"

"My *friend*," Henry corrected, and I felt my face turning seven shades of red.

"Of course, of course," Uncle Marty said. "Foolish of me to presume. Well, Barbara Anne asked me to find out about your new house, Henry. And I've got some information that—"

"You TOLD him?" Henry asked.

"Not about the ghosts, no," I said.

"Well, you have now!" Henry yelled.

A few people looked up then, and one lady even shushed us.

"By the time you're through, everybody in Seattle will know."

"Henry," Martin said. "I think you really might want to know what I've discovered. It's quite interesting, actually. And I assure you I won't say a word to anyone about . . . the other bit. Scout's honor."

Uncle Marty raised his hand in some sort of ancient Boy Scout salute. He had a smile on his face and cookie crumbs on his sweater. Honestly, how could you get mad at somebody who looked that harmless?

"I want to know whatever she knows," Henry said.

"That's the spirit!" Martin said. "Well, Henry, to begin with, it seems your new house is listed on the National Register of Historic Places."

"Sophie says that's because it's over a hundred years old," Henry said.

"That's right," said Martin. "Its age alone would put it on the register. But it also turns out that the original owner was Dr. Thomas Winterson."

"Winterson?" I asked, looking at Henry. I wondered if he was thinking what I was. Was Henry picturing the cursive handwriting inside the little book from the trunk? *This book belongs to P. Winterson*, it said.

"Yes," Martin said. "And Winterson is quite an interesting fellow. Let's take a walk, and I'll show you."

We passed endless rows of books and people studying. Then Uncle Marty reached a tiny glass room. There was no secret code to unlock the door, but it did require a key. And once we were inside, we had to put on white cotton gloves.

"Gloves?" Henry asked.

"It's required," Martin told him, "for handling anything in the archive."

Once we put them on, Uncle Marty put a big, white cardboard box on the table. Then he lifted out a pile of thin, yellowish paper and a black leather book.

"What is it?" Henry asked.

"A journal," Martin said, handing the book to Henry. "Dr. Winterson's journal. He began it near the start of the First World War and concluded it just as the war—and the worst of the pandemic—were ending."

Henry was holding the book, but all three of us were reading the small cursive handwriting.

Monday, October 21, 1918
Another long day of tending to patients and providing the experimental serum to as many as we were able. Commissioner McBride seems convinced

that the pandemic has at last reached its peak and will
now begin to abate. I wish I shared his confidence.
Elizabeth is doing the best she can at home with the
boys, but they grow restless with nothing to do all day
and have no real motivation to keep up with their
studies now that the schools have been closed.

"Pandemic?" I asked.

"From Latin," Martin said. "Meaning 'all people.' It was a virus, a horribly deadly one. No one knows exactly how many people it killed, but the estimate is fifty million or more all over the world. Three percent of the world's population. Worse than the war. Nobody knows for certain where it started, but it spread fast. And the soldiers, in their military camps . . . well, it was bad there. Crowded. The soldiers were malnourished. Hygiene was poor."

"So he was a soldier?" Henry asked. "This Dr. Winterson?"

"No," Martin said. "He was a civilian doctor. Here in Seattle. Soldiers just brought the virus home. It was highly contagious. Imagine this: Every time someone who was sick sneezed or coughed, millions of virus particles could spread to anyone nearby. It was easy to catch and impossible to cure. They handed out masks, passed laws against spitting, told people to stay home, but there were no good ways to treat it, really. Some of them died directly when the virus ruined their lungs. Most of them got a secondary infection, pneumonia. And that's what did them in."

"That's awful," I said.

Uncle Marty looked at his watch. "It's time for my break," he said. "Why don't I take you two out for a bite to eat?"

And Henry and I were glad to leave.

CHAPTER FIFTEEN

THE AWFUL TRUTH

Uncle Marty decided he needed to "stretch his legs," so the three of us walked down to the market. It was good to be out in the air, to see people laughing, buying flowers, sampling fruit. We grabbed some sandwiches and sat on a small patch of grass facing the water. We watched the boats in the distance, the gulls swooping. We talked of more cheerful things.

"Have you been on the Ferris wheel?" Martin asked Henry.

"Sophie took me, and Alice, a few weeks ago."

"So she's not all bad, this stepmother of yours," Martin said.

"I guess not," Henry answered.

"And the new school is working out?"

Henry nodded and chewed on his sandwich.

"Well, I can see you've done a fine job of making new friends," he said. And he smiled at me.

When we finished, Uncle Marty asked if we wanted to continue with the journal. "I could walk you to the bus stop," he offered. "If it's been enough for one day."

Henry surprised me when he said, "I need to hear the rest of it."

And so we trudged up the hill. We returned to the library. We went back—to the journal and the little glass room, to 1918.

Wednesday, October 23, 1918

It seems all we do is search for more space, more beds, more nurses, and more supplies to care for all who are ill. The courthouse is in use, and now we look toward other sectors too for assistance. Visited our pastor today to see if the church might be temporarily converted, as services have now been banned anyway. The kitchen is large, and the Red Cross still has enough supplies to assist us. Will return this evening to see to the arrangements. The streets are empty. Even the Green Lake trolley is not as crowded as

before, and everyone's eyes (above their masks) seem
full of fear.

"Why can't they go to church?" Henry asked.

"Too many people," Martin said. "They were afraid the flu would spread. They called it a 'crowd disease.' They closed the schools, churches, movie theaters. Every large public gathering was canceled. It was too dangerous. And the hospitals couldn't keep up, so they had to look for other places where they could care for the people who caught it."

"So he's going to build a hospital?" I asked.

"Not exactly," Martin said. "He's talking about making a hospital, a temporary one, inside a church by bringing in cots and supplies and medical staff. That's what they did at the courthouse too. Everything was coming to a stop."

"Like a snow day?" I asked.

Uncle Marty smiled a sad smile. "Well, they were indoors, if that's what you mean. And after a time, there was no school and no chance to play outdoors or go to a movie. But more than being bored, they must have been afraid. Especially the adults, who knew what might happen. This next entry mentions the temporary hospitals. Listen," Martin said. And he read aloud to us.

Friday, October 25, 1918

The church has been set up, and beds there fill as quickly as they did at the courthouse. We have been largely spared so far, losing only a few of those we know directly—Mrs. McAdams, who worshipped at our church, passed away a week ago. The grocer's wife, Elizabeth tells me, is another victim. But then, this morning, as I passed the Pritchett house, the shades were being drawn. By evening, the white crepe hung near the bell. One of the twins must surely have succumbed. We must go pay our respects, or at least drop a note once we are certain what has happened. How I dread mentioning this to Elizabeth, worried as she is about our own two boys. Miss Leary tells me her family is well, which is a relief. Don't know what I would say to Phillip and Edgar if we lost Constance or Candace.

"Stop for a second," Henry said.

"What is it?" Martin asked.

Henry and I looked at one another. There they were. All the names, linked together, not just Winterson, which had struck us both the moment Uncle Marty had said it, but Constance Leary and Phillip and Edgar. Was that what Edgar had been whispering through Henry's radio? Not "wind" and "stone" but "Winterson"?

"Phillip and Edgar," Henry said, his voice sounding shaky. "They're Dr. Winterson's—"

"His sons," Martin said. "The younger one, Edgar . . . well, I can keep reading, but . . ."

But we already knew the awful truth. We both realized that Edgar must have died from the flu, even though neither of us wanted to say it. Not out loud.

"Are you all right?" Martin asked Henry.

Henry nodded, but he didn't look good. I touched his forehead with my wrist the way my mom does. "He's burning hot," I told Uncle Marty. "Henry, I think you have a fever."

"I think we'd better finish this another day," Martin said.

Henry looked horrible on the ride home—pale and tired—and he'd started to cough. I felt awful for dragging him out. What made it even worse was reading the journal. In our world, Edgar had always been dead, but on those pages, he was just a little boy, a real, living little boy whose father had no idea that he was about to lose him.

CHAPTER SIXTEEN

QUESTIONS

Henry was absent when I got to school on Monday. I wasn't surprised, of course. I knew he was still sick, but it was disappointing. All I really wanted to do was talk to him about Edgar. We knew so much more now, and it was the best secret I'd ever had with anyone. Well, maybe you couldn't really call it a secret anymore, since Renee and Zack knew too, and, of course, Uncle Marty. But somehow I still felt Edgar belonged to Henry and me—which didn't stop me from telling Renee and Zack about Uncle Marty's research.

"There's a book written about him?" Zack asked.

We were standing at the far edge of the playground, where no one else could hear.

"Not a book," I said. "It's a journal—like a diary—that his dad wrote."

"And he died?" Renee asked. "Edgar?"

"Of course he died," Zack said. "That's the first step if you're a ghost."

"He had influenza. It's like pneumonia," I said.

"I hope that's not what Henry has," Renee said.

"I thought he had bronchitis," Zack said.

"Hey, do you think he caught it from Edgar?" Renee asked. "The pneumonia?"

"Hundred-year-old pneumonia germs?" I asked. "I don't think so. Dust doesn't even have time to form in that house with Sophie around."

"Sometimes they keep them on purpose," Zack said. "Viruses. They put them in a freezer in a lab somewhere, like Popsicles. And then they have to hope they don't escape."

"Well, Henry's room's as cold as a freezer," Renee said. "And I'm never going back there again."

"Why not? It's more fun than finding out everything at the library," Zack said.

And that gave me an idea. "We don't always need the library," I said. "I have a plan."

"Do you think we should have called first?" Renee asked as she and Zack and I stood at Henry's front door that night.

"Now you ask this?" I said. "I was just about to ring the bell."

"Isn't it going to look suspicious?" Renee asked.

"No," I said. "We're bringing him his homework."

"I guess," she said. "But it doesn't really take three people to carry one math book."

"She has a point," Zack said, but then he pushed the bell anyway.

"Hey, you're early," Sophie was saying as she opened the door. And then she seemed to realize that it was us, just as we were recognizing that she expected somebody else. Somebodies, actually. Her book club, to be specific.

"We brought Henry's homework over," I said. "We thought it would be fun to surprise him."

"Thank you," Sophie said. "That's so thoughtful of you. I'd invite you in to say hello, but—"

Fortunately, Henry's dad appeared over her shoulder then and invited us all in anyhow.

"Just for a minute," he said to Sophie.

Upstairs, the three of us told Henry why we were really there. "You guys can't set up a Ouija board here," he said. "You can't even stay. *We* can't even stay. Sophie just told me not to leave my room, and my dad's going to hide in the basement. Alice only gets to show her face downstairs because she promised to serve cookies."

"Wow," I said. "They must really want privacy. What do they talk about at this book club?"

"Who knows?" Henry said. "All I know is that they laugh a lot. And they get all the cookies."

"Oh well," Renee said. "I guess we better go."

But even though Renee was willing to forget the whole thing, Zack and I were more determined.

"Wait," Zack said. "Didn't you say your ghost guy haunts the school too?"

"Yeah," I said. "The music room."

"Perfect," Zack said. "Let's take the Ouija board to the music room."

"How are we getting in?" I asked. "Breaking and entering is a felony, in case you haven't heard."

"They don't arrest kids," Zack said.

"Of course they do," Henry said.

"Well, we're not going to do breaking and entering. We're just going to do entering," Zack said. "It's Family Fitness Night. We can get in through the gym like everybody else and then go up to the music room."

"This is a terrible idea," Henry said. "Count me out."

"Listen," Zack said. "None of us would even be doing this if it weren't for you. We're trying to help."

Ah, guilt. Always a good strategy. And I thought it would work on Henry, but it didn't. Not at first.

"You're not going for me," Henry said. "You just want to play around with the Ouija board."

"Okay," Zack said. "I admit it. But you have to come. We need your help."

"Zack's right," I said. "You're the one who knows Edgar. You're the one he'll want to talk to."

"Yeah? Well, *I'm* the one my dad is going to want to talk to if I leave the house without permission."

"How will he know?" Renee said. "You told us he was going to the basement, right? Couldn't you just go down there, tell him your friends are leaving, and say good night? Then we sneak you out."

Pretty devious, coming from Renee. I was impressed.

"Great," Henry said. "How am I sneaking back in?"

"Easy," said Zack. "Just don't lose your keys this time."

"If nothing else works," I pointed out, "you could always fake sleepwalking."

"Brilliant, Barbara Anne," Henry said.

But he got up and headed down to the basement to say good night to his dad. I grabbed a sweatshirt out of Henry's closet so he could throw it on over his pajamas. Then we waited until Alice and Sophie were in the kitchen getting the snacks. That's when all of us snuck back down the stairs.

The walk to school that night seemed superlong, but maybe it was because my backpack was so heavy. It was jammed full of stuff. The Ouija board, of course, was the main thing. That's right. I still had it, which might have been wrong, I suppose. But going after a ghost isn't like trying to catch a butterfly with a net. You never know what you might need. Besides, Monica would get the Ouija board back when Edgar left. Who knew when that might be, but like my grandmother always says, "It's better to owe you than to cheat you out of it."

The Ouija board wasn't the only thing inside my backpack, though. There was a bunch of smaller stuff in there too: a compass, a thermometer, a notebook, candles, matches, and some rope. (Yeah, I'm not sure what the rope was for either. Even if Edgar was there, it wasn't like we were going to tie him up.) I was prepared, that's the real point, and I knew what I was looking for.

Here are the signs that a ghost might be near:

- Lights that flicker for no reason or bulbs that suddenly blow out
- Strange shadows or movements in your peripheral vision
- Noises—like music or whispers—that you can't find the source of

- Changes in temperature—usually a sudden breeze or cold spot
- Unusual scents—like the lilacs in Henry's dream

And don't bother chanting or asking them to appear. Ghosts come and go as they please. They're the ones in charge, and they know it.

Anyway, it was pitch-black outside as the four of us made our way to the school. I felt scared but excited too. This was just like those ghost hunter shows on TV. I could picture myself becoming famous this way. I would have my own office and everything. Terrified people would sit in chairs in front of my huge desk and burst into tears. "I don't know what to do!" they would sob. And I would hand them Kleenex. And my business card.

Barbara Anne Klein
Ghost Hunter

I was picturing the four of us inside the school, our shadows stretching along the walls as we crept toward the dark music room. Doors would slowly creak open and—

Then Zack opened the gym door, and bright lights and Hawaiian music sprang out. Family Fitness Night! Our gym teacher was there in a flowered shirt and a fake grass skirt, and everybody inside—little kids, chubby dads, *everybody*—was having some sort of hula hoop contest. It totally, totally, totally ruined the mood!

Upstairs, things were more what I imagined—quiet and dark. We started down the hallway, but right away I made everyone stop. "Wait!" I said. And I took out my notebook and handed it to Renee. "Write this down. Date: November 19th. Time: approximately 8:33. Slight wind. Clear skies."

"Clear skies?" Renee said. "We're in a hallway."

"Not here," I said. "Outside."

"Who cares?" Henry complained. "What is this, anyway? A weather report?"

"I'm trying to do this right!" I said.

"I'm not sure we should do this at all," Renee said.

It was so like her to try to chicken out at the last minute. "Obviously, we're doing this, Renee," I said. "We're already in the *middle* of doing this." Honestly.

"Well, I'm using my flashlight," Renee said before we even reached the stairs that led up to the music room. Then she started digging through her backpack.

"Hurry up," Zack said.

"Here," I said. And I handed Renee a thick white candle. "You can hold this instead. The flame attracts the spirits."

"Oh, great, Barbara Anne," Henry said. "Let's just burn down the whole school while we're at it."

"Well, it's better than her mini flashlight. You can't see anything with that!" I was starting to get nervous myself; I was remembering what happened the night of the school play—with the piano. I lit the candle and handed it to Renee. Then we continued down the hallway. The candle was flickering, lighting up random sections of this jungle mural we painted last fall in art class. We made it only a few feet before Renee let out a bloodcurdling scream. All of us jumped about a foot in the air.

"What?" Zack yelled.

"A rat!" she said. "I think I just saw a rat! It went behind that garbage can in the corner!"

"Calm down!" Zack said.

To be fair, I should say that Zack was never going to understand, because he has a rat for a pet and is always telling everyone how clean and smart they are. I, for one, got it. The screaming, that is. Not a fan of rodents myself. I hate rats. And mice too. Those tiny, pointed teeth. Those teeny-tiny, supersharp claws. Nope. Not for me. Give me a dog or a cat anytime. Nothing that can escape its cage and scurry.

"Which way did it go?" I asked Renee.

"That way!" she said, pointing at the hallway ahead.

Henry took one look at us and said, "It's okay. Let me go first."

And so we waited while Henry went ahead alone. Henry—who still had on the dinosaur-patterned pajama pants he was wearing when we snuck out of his house. In a minute or two, he motioned to the rest of us. "It's okay," he said. "I think it's gone."

We kept going then. But Renee still looked petrified.

Then Zack opened the door that led to the staircase up to the music room. Every stair seemed to squeak, and the candle tossed weird shadows along the walls.

"I don't like this," Renee said. And nobody could blame her. She was only naming what we all felt.

The music room, when we reached it, was colder, draftier, than the hallway below. It was like we had climbed a whole mountain instead of a flight of stairs. Renee held the candle up like a torch and stepped forward into the darkness. "Where should we do it?" she asked. "Where should we set up?"

It wasn't like a regular classroom. So there were no desks. We usually sat on the floor, or on folding chairs that were packed away in the closet. All we found now was a dark, open space. At the edge of the room, I could just make out the shape of the piano in the moonlight.

"Put the board near the window," Zack said. "So we can see."

"Good idea," I said. Then I told Renee to hand me the candle.

"Don't blow it out!" she said.

"I'm not going to blow it out. I have a holder," I said, pulling my mom's brass candlestick out of the bottom of my backpack.

"Hey," Zack said. "This is just like that murder game. You've got a rope and a candlestick. All we need now is a wrench."

"Very funny," I said. "Just help me set up the board, or we're going to be here all night."

Henry, Renee, Zack, and I arranged ourselves on the floor, cross-legged, in front of the window. Between the candle burning on the piano above us and a bit of moonlight, we could see pretty well. I explained how it worked, and we all put our fingers on the planchette.

"How soon will it move?" Zack asked. In his voice, I heard the mix of nervousness and excitement that all of us were feeling.

"I don't know," I whispered. "We ask a question, and then we wait. Just remember not to push it. Ready?"

Henry and Zack nodded right away, but I could tell Renee was having second thoughts again.

"Renee?" I asked. "Are you ready?"

"I'm not sure," she answered. "But go ahead."

I looked around at their faces, glowing in the dim light. Then I took a deep breath, to gather my courage, and I asked, "Edgar, why are you here?"

At first there was nothing. The room was so quiet I could hear the others breathing. But then the planchette started to shift, just like last time. Slowly at first, but then faster and faster, it spelled out a name: C-O-N-S-T-A-N-C-E.

"Miss Leary?" Henry asked.

The planchette pulled to the corner of the board, to the word YES.

"But why?" I asked. "What do you want from her?"

We waited then. Nothing.

"It's not working," Henry said. "He's gone."

"Don't give up," I told him. "Edgar," I said. "We don't understand. Why are you here?"

"I'm scared," Renee said.

"It's okay," I said. "You can do this. Just don't lift your fingers."

Then he did it again. Edgar pulled our hands toward the letters of her name: C-O-N-S-T-A-N-C-E.

And then the planchette began to move again: G-O-O-D-B-Y-E.

I was about to lift my fingers, about to give up, when Renee's voice stopped me. "Wait!" she yelled. "Edgar!"

She sounded sad. Desperate. We all stared at her.

"I need to ask him something," she said.

"Go ahead," I told her.

"Edgar?" Renee asked in a small, trembling voice. "Is my mom all right?"

The planchette pulled—right away—to YES. Even if I didn't understand yet what the rest of it had meant, I was glad that Renee had gotten her answer. I hoped it would help.

"Ask him something else," Zack said to Renee.

She shook her head. "It's no use. He's gone."

"I guess you're right," Henry said. "Or maybe the 'good-bye' is somehow about Constance."

I didn't understand exactly what Henry meant. All I knew was that the room seemed suddenly crowded, full of strange energy. The whispering between the four of us was a buzzing noise, frantic and scary, like bees in a jar.

And then I saw it. Behind their heads, on the window, a small circle of fogged-up glass formed and then faded, and then re-formed—in a slow, hypnotic rhythm. It was as if somebody outside in the dark, on the old iron fire escape, was *breathing* on the window. I watched it, mesmerized. There was nothing I wanted to ask, nothing I wanted to know. It was obvious then that Edgar was still there with us, and all I wanted to do now was leave.

"Let's get out of here!" I said, and at the same moment, a

cold gust of wind blew through the room. The candle went out, and the four of us were alone in the dark.

Edgar was gone.

We were quiet, at first, on the walk home. Talking to Edgar had been strange, even before Renee brought her mom into the whole thing. Don't get me wrong. I felt really sorry for her. I just wasn't sure what to say.

"I'm glad you got to ask—about your mom," I told her finally.

"All I've ever wanted is to talk to her again," she said. "Even one time."

The rest of us were silent. We just moved together down the empty sidewalk in the moonlight until Renee said, "There's this phone booth in Japan. It's called the wind phone. Somebody made it after a tsunami. And you can go there and say whatever you want. You can talk to whoever you lost. I want to go there someday."

"I bet you will," Zack said.

Then Henry asked, "What do you think he wants? From Constance?"

"Maybe she killed him," Zack said. "And Edgar wants revenge."

"Stop it!" Renee said.

"No. They were friends," Henry said.

"Barbara Anne's our friend, and sometimes I want to kill her," Zack said.

"Henry's right," I said, ignoring Zack. "We saw a journal in the library the other day. Edgar's father wrote it, and he mentioned Constance."

"Then maybe," Renee said. "Maybe Edgar just came back to say goodbye."

CHAPTER SEVENTEEN

THANKSGIVING

At school the next day, everything was back to normal, and that wasn't entirely a good thing. It turned out that Halloween wasn't the only holiday Ms. Biniam felt like spoiling. She didn't seem to understand that Thanksgiving was mainly a day to sleep late and eat pie.

"We are really a fortunate group," she said that morning. "And I've been thinking that we might celebrate our good fortune by doing something for our neighbors—in honor of the holiday."

"Uh-oh," said Zack. "This doesn't sound good."

"So I'd like us all to find a partner and list some things you might do. Some ideas—for community service."

We looked at her blankly.

"Maybe we can start by talking about what that term means. 'Community service.' Zack?"

"I think my uncle had to do it once. Isn't it like when a judge forces criminals to pick up trash on the side of the road?"

Everyone laughed. Ms. Biniam sighed.

And then she started writing a list of possible projects on the board and assigning each of us a partner. My partner was Renee, and her idea was that we should raise money to buy food. Then we could pack it into little baskets and deliver it to old people or hungry people or hungry old people, I guess. So we made a sign that said KIDS FOR CHANGE, and for the next few days we put out a jar on a folding table after school. I thought I was working pretty hard on the whole thing, but Renee didn't seem especially grateful. Just because I said hello to a couple of people, she complained that all I "ever did" was talk. Actually, all we ever did was stand there looking bored while everybody else walked right past us on their way home.

"We need to get their attention somehow," I said. "This sign isn't working at all. Maybe it should just say 'Give Us Your Change!'"

"Barbara Anne! You're kidding, right?"

She looked horrified, so I said I was. "Yes, of course. Who would do that?"

I would. I totally would. And I bet it would work too.

"We need turkeys!" I yelled. I felt inspired suddenly. "Help us buy some turkeys!"

Renee did not appreciate this approach either. In fact, she clapped her hand over my mouth to demonstrate how much she loved the idea.

"What? We do. We need turkeys."

"Hungry people are not a joke, you idiot," Renee said. "And besides, we're not giving them turkeys."

"We're not putting turkeys in a Thanksgiving food basket?" I asked. "That seems like the whole point!"

"We can't," Renee said. "I already got the baskets, and they're not big enough. Besides, Barbara Anne, a turkey? They're huge and heavy and *greasy*."

"Then what are we putting in?"

"I don't know. I was thinking pumpkin bread."

"Pumpkin bread? You expect me to knock on some stranger's door and just give them pumpkin bread? When the rest of us are eating turkeys?"

"The food pantry says they can give us some of their extra stuff to add in. They've got tuna fish—"

"Tuna fish! That's even worse. Nobody likes tuna fish."

"Lots of people like tuna fish, Barbara Anne. You're not the expert on what food everyone likes."

"Hey!" I called to a little first grader who was passing by. "Can I ask you a question?"

"I'm looking for my mom," the girl said.

"A quick question," I said.

"Barbara Anne!" Renee said. "She's trying to find her mom. What's wrong with you?"

I ignored Renee and bent down low to get on the little girl's level. "Do you like tuna fish?" I asked. "You know, the oily fish stuff that comes in a can?"

The girl stuck her tongue out and ran away.

"See?" I said. "She hates it."

"I think she hates you," Renee said, and she grabbed the change jar away from me.

"I'm going to get some stuff for a new sign," I told her, and I marched off.

When I got to the classroom, I didn't go in right away. The sound of voices stopped me.

"Zack has made terrific progress," I heard Biniam say. "He's really learning to think before he acts."

And then a woman's voice said, "That's what we're hoping. That's what the counselor says."

"Well," Biniam said. "It's a parent's job to worry, but Zack has come a long way. You should be proud."

"We are," the other voice said. It had to be Zack's mom. "We know he's doing better. We just don't want him to be asked to leave another school."

"I understand," Ms. Biniam said. "But that was, what? Two years ago? Zack's doing well here."

They were walking toward the door then. I pretended to go to my locker. I forgot all about the sign and the poster board. Instead, I watched while Zack's mom gave Ms. Biniam a hug. I remembered all the times Zack would count to ten, or walk outside for a drink of water. And it surprised me a little, how glad I was—to realize how much Zack must have changed, to see how much his mom loved him.

I knew Zack's secret now, and I knew that I'd never mention it. Zack wasn't the only one who was growing up.

Thanksgiving was getting close, and I wasn't sure Renee and I would be ready. Things weren't going any better for Henry. Biniam had him working with Zack, and they were part of a bigger group that was supposed to visit old people at an assisted-living place.

"You've got it easy!" I told him at lunch. "One visit? That's it? I would trade with you any day."

"We have to *perform*," Henry said. "Like a talent show that they can watch."

"So? How hard can that be?"

"I have Zack as my partner," Henry said. "He wants to play the guitar while we sing."

"Okay," I said.

"No," Henry said. "Not okay. Not okay at all. Do you know what he wants to sing? 'Dust in the Wind.' I'm not singing that! To a bunch of old people who might die in thirty seconds? 'All we are is dust in the wind'?"

"Maybe you can still switch groups," I said. "I hear Alonzo's doing a coat drive."

"Already asked," Henry said. "No switching. They're really excited we're coming."

"Well, maybe you can just change songs," I said.

"Zack says that's the only song his dad's taught him so far," Henry said. "I'm doomed," he added, and he put his head down on the table while I started to laugh.

Things went a little better for Renee and me. It turned out the baskets worked fine and even looked pretty cute. They did have the bread, but also fruit and nuts, all tied up with a ribbon and everything. (Not a can of tuna fish in sight. Thank you very much.)

I know it might be vain to say so, but I looked nice too. My hair was clipped back with my favorite red barrette, and I was wearing my favorite dress, also red. And at the last minute, I put on the locket. The locket from the trunk. That was a small mistake, because when my mother saw it, she wanted to know where it came from.

"I found it," I said. And that was true enough.

"Found it where?" she asked. That's the thing about my mom. She's very big on follow-up questions. And I was not ready for this one, so that's when the fibbing started.

"At school," I said.

She sighed. "Barbara Anne, you can't just keep something because you find it. Not something special like that. It may have sentimental value to someone. You have an obligation to look for the owner."

I figured I was already in pretty deep, so I just kept going. "Oh, I know that," I said. "I hung up a sign at the lost-and-found. And I put my name and room number on it. I know I'll have to give it back. If it belongs to somebody."

There. Problem solved. As long as my mother did not stop by the lost-and-found anytime soon.

"Just don't lose it," she warned me.

And everything was fine then—for a while. My mom was taking me to deliver the baskets, and she had the list of who was supposed to get them in her bag. She would slide it out and announce the name, and my job was to plug the address into her phone so we didn't get lost. It was fun. For a while.

And then she said, "Oh, we don't need directions for this one. It's on Henry's street."

"What's the name?" I asked.

I think I already knew. Dread had already begun to

descend. My stomach hurt before the words were even out of her mouth.

"Leary," my mother said. "Constance Leary."

Why? Why oh why oh why? Why me?

"Isn't she that nice old lady who goes to Henry's church?" she asked. "The one you raked leaves for?"

How to answer this? "No, Mom. She's not. She has a hideous, cloudy white eyeball and some sort of creepy, hypnotic hold over Henry."

Sure. That's what I said. Not in a million years. Here's what I said: "You know, Mom, she's really old. So old I think she just sleeps most of the time. Maybe we should just leave the basket on her porch. You know. So the doorbell doesn't wake her up."

I was impressed with my own skill. Houdini couldn't have wiggled out of a tight spot any faster than that. Unfortunately, my mother was not going for it. She did this little thing she does, this slow nod/raised eyebrow combination, which is never a good sign.

"Really?" she asked, and she said it way too slowly. "You know what I think?"

I held my breath—literally—and waited to find out.

"I think what Miss Leary could really use—even more than this thoughtful basket—is a chance to chat with someone."

"I guess we could—"

"No, no, no. Not *we*, Barbara Anne. You. I'm going to park the car and walk down to get a coffee. That'll give you and Miss Leary a chance to visit."

And that was it. My fate was sealed.

I stood there on the porch with the wind whipping through my hair and leaves skittering across the steps. I knocked, maybe not as loudly as I could have, but that was beside the point. Then I stood there, counting the seconds, trying to decide how long I had to wait before it would be fair to tell my mother that nobody was home. The helper lady answered on five. She was really excited to see me too, couldn't wait to tell Miss Leary. "Constance, we have a visitor."

The entryway was small. Two steps in, and I could see her—Constance Leary. She sat in the corner of the living room in a dark dress, just staring at me with her sharp-featured face and strange eyes. She reminded me of a crow, really. And I know everybody says how intelligent crows are, but that's never made me like them. They can remember your face; did you know that? And that just seems like more than a bird should be able to do. So it's that and how loud they are and how sometimes they swoop down toward people and even peck them in the head and how *big* the flocks get sometimes when they land on the telephone wires near the playground. She looked like that. Just sitting there, silent, but also like any minute she might flap her huge dark sleeves and scream, "CAW, caw, caw!"

"Oh, what a lovely basket! Go on in," the helper lady said. "I'll get you some cider. You like cider, right?"

I wished I could follow her into the kitchen so that I could see what it actually looked like in there instead of just making it up in my head. Because what I was imagining was some huge vat, or cauldron thingy, of cider that they just kept warm on the stove to serve to any unsuspecting children whose mean mothers forced them to stop by. Possibly poisoned cider. (Probably poisoned.)

"Thank you," I said. "I do like cider." Because how could it help to be rude now that I was at their mercy?

I walked toward Miss Leary with the basket over my arm. I felt like Little Red Riding Hood again. My knees were shaking. Miss Leary had a small table set up in front of her wheelchair, and she was shuffling a deck of cards. She motioned me to pull up a chair.

"Ah," she said. "You're just in time. I was about to start telling my fortune, and you can read the cards. Are you a good reader?"

"Excellent," I said.

She dealt the cards out onto a board, a mat, that had categories like Wishes, Moon, Happiness. Then she handed me a book, and it was my job to explain what each card meant. I didn't know a lot about fortune-telling, but one thing I did know was that sometimes you got bad news. The top row didn't look too scary, but I was definitely hoping my mom would reappear before we got to row three, where the categories shifted over to things like Trouble, Disappointment, and—the big one—Death. I was just there to drop off pumpkin bread. If we got to that square and things didn't go well, I would just have to see something else in her future. Maybe a puppy.

Once we got going, I started to enjoy the game. It turned out I did have to cheat here and there, though. Some of the messages just did not seem to fit Miss Leary. I couldn't predict the future, but I really didn't think she'd have a marriage proposal by the end of the year. So I told her instead that she'd be invited to a wedding.

"That's so exciting," she said. "We've never gotten that one before. Write it down, please. Write it down in the notebook so I won't forget."

I sat across from her, holding the little book, trying to remember exactly what I had said so that I could record it for her. And while I was staring at the page, Miss Leary was concentrating on me.

"You look so pretty," she said. "All dressed up. Can I see that locket you're wearing?"

I took it off and handed it to her, and she turned it over in her hands while I wrote her fortune down in my best handwriting. Suddenly I realized how foolish I'd been, and

I was afraid to look up. Everything in the trunk seemed connected to her somehow. Her name was in the yearbook and in Dr. Winterson's journal. For all I knew, the locket might be hers. And now she would know I'd stolen it. And snooped around trying to find out more about her too, from a Ouija board no less. When I finally found the courage to lift my head, I saw that Miss Leary had opened the locket and was looking at the picture inside.

"How did you know him?" I asked.

And she smiled. "Edgar was my best friend. My child-hood sweetheart."

CHAPTER EIGHTEEN

LONG AGO AND FAR AWAY

Constance (she told me to call her that) showed me other pictures of Edgar. A class picture where their faces were almost too tiny to pick out, and another of Edgar and his brother standing in front of an old-fashioned car.

"He used to call me Freckles," Constance said.

"I saw that," I said. "Henry and I found a yearbook, your high school yearbook, in the attic."

"That must have belonged to Phillip," Constance told me. "His brother. Edgar was gone by the time we graduated. I never forgot him, though. He was a wonderful little boy! A true friend. But he could be a devil too. Loved to play tricks. He'd hide behind a tree and jump out at me as I walked to school. He pulled more than one prank. He was my partner in crime. We could play checkers for hours. He usually won. Beat me at marbles too, almost every day in the fourth grade! His parents always tried to get him to be more studious, practice harder. He was a wonderful pianist. A prodigy, really. I used to have his piano for a time. Before I donated it—to your school."

"The piano in the music room at school is yours?" I asked her.

"I suppose so. But I'll always think of it as Edgar's."

I thought then of the night of the play, of the keys moving all on their own. Should I tell her that Edgar loved the piano still, that even now he played it some nights in the darkness of the empty music room?

"You know," she was saying, "Edgar was only eleven years old when he died. The flu. Same as my sister, Candy. Threw a dark cloud over me for a long time. It was the end of my childhood, really. You can't imagine how many people we lost. They couldn't even keep up. And everything was about the flu. We even sang about it when we skipped rope."

"Like a jump rope rhyme?" I asked.

"Yes," she said. And then she recited it.

> *I had a little bird,*
> *Its name was Enza.*
> *I opened up the window,*
> *And in-flu-enza.*

"Henry's uncle Marty told us about it," I said. "The flu. But there's still something I don't get. I know it was hard to cure, but some people survived. And Edgar's father was a doctor. Why couldn't he do something? He had medicine, didn't he?"

"Nothing magic. Nothing that would help, I'm afraid. They tried a vaccine, but it didn't work. And more foolish things. Patent medicine full of sarsaparilla. One lady in Oregon took to telling everyone to eat more onions! Nothing worked. And they blamed us! Said it was partly fear that caused it. Can you imagine? Things slowed down when the war ended, but even then, it was a couple of years before it stopped completely. About all they could do was keep us at home. They closed the schools, made us stay indoors. Edgar was fit to be tied. All he wanted was to go outside and play. Such a sad thing! A lively little boy like that spending his last days on Earth looking out the window, trapped inside. It hurts me even now to think of it. He was supposed to come for my birthday, but his mother wouldn't even let him come across, wouldn't let him out of the house once the schools closed. All he could do was wave to me—from the window."

She was quiet for a minute. Then she asked me, "Why does this interest you so? And how do you know about Dr. Winterson?"

"It's all because of Henry," I said. "My friend Henry. Your neighbor."

"Yes," she said. "Sophie's boy. Does Henry take an interest in history?"

"Not exactly," I said. "Edgar . . . well, Edgar sort of *visits* Henry."

"I'm not surprised," she said calmly.

But I was shocked by her reaction. And also relieved. Except for that slip with Uncle Marty in the library, I'd never told a grown-up before, about the ghosts. I wasn't sure what to expect. "You're not?" I asked. "You've seen him too?"

"No," she said. "Since he died, I've only been able to see him in photographs. But there *are* times, when I've been ill or unhappy, I suppose. That's when I feel him with me. I sense his presence."

"You called Henry by Edgar's name," I said. "When the two of you were playing checkers."

"Did I?" she asked.

"Henry doesn't remember it either," I said. "But he's been acting pretty strange, off and on, ever since I met him."

"Well," she said. "Isn't he fortunate to have a friend like you, who notices and worries."

"I'm the lucky one," I said. "He's the best friend I ever had. The first real one. It's kind of hard to admit this, but not everybody at school likes me. Some of them think I'm kind of obnoxious, I think."

Constance laughed. "It's not always easy being the smartest one in the class, is it?"

The doorbell rang then.

"That must be your mother," Constance said. "Come to collect you." And she handed me the locket.

"I'm sorry I took your locket, Constance," I said. "I didn't know."

"Oh, it isn't mine, dear. It belonged to Edgar's mother, Elizabeth."

There wasn't time to say more about it, so I slipped the locket back around my neck and rushed off to get my coat. Constance thanked me again for the basket, and we said our goodbyes.

After I talked to Constance, I decided that I should go back—to finish reading Dr. Winterson's diary. So the next day, I told my mom that I wanted to go to the library.

"The library's not even open today," she said.

"The downtown library's open," I told her.

"Why do you need to go all the way into the city?" she wanted to know. "Can't it wait until Monday?"

I was all set to tell her that I needed things for my project, but I didn't have to because my dad volunteered to take me. He had to do some stuff at his office anyway.

"See you right back here in a half hour," he said as I got out of the car.

"An hour," I said.

"Okay, okay," he said. "One hour." And he pulled back out into traffic.

Uncle Marty unlocked the room for me and gave me the white gloves. Then he let me stay there by myself to read the rest of the diary. The last few entries were short, and even though I knew what was coming, the news Dr. Winterson shared was harsh. This time, I sat all alone in the little glass room. I opened the black leather book with no title, and this is what I saw:

> *Wednesday, November 6, 1918*
>
> *Our beloved boy is gone. Elizabeth washed and dressed him herself and readied him for the journey, though I begged her not to. We hear the church bells tolling all day, it seems; so many know this same sadness.*

> *Monday, November 11, 1918*
>
> *Last night in France the war was ended, and this morning I have lost my dear Elizabeth, whose illness followed close on the heels of Edgar's. The city is alive*

with celebration—bands and parades. Tonight, there
will be fireworks downtown. But here, for Phillip and
me, the worst has just begun, and I cannot imagine
how we will survive it.

Monday, November 25, 1918
 I have given the piano away. To the Learys.
Perhaps their darling Constance can learn to play.
Phillip and I cannot bear to see it anyway now that
Edgar will never play it again.

When I finished the journal, I stopped to tell Uncle
Marty goodbye and to thank him. At the last second, I'm
not sure why, I said, "Mr. Corrigan?"

"Yes?"

"I have one more question."

"About the journal?"

"No," I said. "Just something I've been wondering, and I
really hope you don't mind if I ask."

"Okay," he said.

"Well, Mr. Corrigan? Do you think . . . I mean, have you
ever . . . Do you believe in ghosts?"

It was hard to ask, but I'm glad I did, because Uncle Marty
had a ghost story of his own. And he is positive ghosts are
real, because he saw one himself. When Uncle Marty was
twelve, his grandfather died. Now, this grandfather was

more like the father in Uncle Marty's house. Anyway, after he died, there were signs of him everywhere: the smell of his pipe tobacco sometimes, and once they found his favorite book lying open by his chair when they got back from visiting friends. Stuff like that. And all of that was weird enough. But one night, Uncle Marty woke up to the sound of the hall clock striking midnight. When he looked out through his open bedroom door, he saw his grandfather pass. The old man's spirit turned its head toward Uncle Marty and smiled.

"I screamed bloody murder," Martin said. "So, yes. I believe in ghosts."

I was afraid Uncle Marty would start asking me questions then, but he didn't. I guess if he'd wanted to know more about what was happening at Henry's house, he would have tried to find out from Henry on our first visit to the library—when I accidentally mentioned the word "ghosts." But Uncle Marty wasn't like that. He didn't expect you to explain more than you wanted to. And I liked that about him. All he did was shake my hand as we said goodbye. "It's been a pleasure helping you, Miss Klein. I admire your curiosity."

On the way home, I couldn't help thinking how sad it was—the journal. I looked out the window as my dad drove. I watched all the people walking by, so busy with their lives. Every one of them, I realized now, was a story I'd never know.

When I got to Henry's house, it looked like nobody was home. No cars in the driveway. But I had to see him, so I took my chances. I ran up the steps and rang the bell.

"Hey," he said when he opened the door. He was smiling, and he looked so glad to see me that I couldn't stop myself. I flung myself at him and hugged him as hard as I could.

"What's that for?" he asked, stepping backward.

"Just for being you," I said.

"Oh-kay," said Henry slowly. He was looking at me like I'd lost my mind.

"Henry, we need to talk. I have a bunch of stuff to tell you."

"I can't now. I'm about to challenge my dad to a game of chess," he said.

"You can do that anytime," I said. "This is really important. It's about Constance, Miss Leary, and Edgar, and—"

"Not now, Barbara Anne. I want to spend time with my dad. And besides, I'm tired of talking about Edgar. And I'm tired of him showing up and scaring me half to death whenever he feels like it."

"What happened now?" I asked him.

"Nothing," Henry said.

But I knew better. "Henry Davis!" I said. "Spill."

And that's when he told me—that the dreams had gotten

more elaborate, more real, that they didn't even seem like dreams anymore. He said it felt more like Edgar's life was always there, just below the surface.

Henry explained that a while ago—when he got sick—things started to . . . overlap.

He said it went in stages. At first, he only heard the music, the piano. But that was how he knew they were there—the other family. He wanted to tell someone, but everyone kept saying that he was sick, that he needed to get some sleep, that he was just dreaming.

"I didn't want to sleep," Henry said. "It felt like every time they made me close my eyes, they were sending me back."

"My grandmother calls those fever dreams, Henry. I've had them too."

"No," he insisted. "You don't understand!"

"Then explain it to me," I said.

"It wasn't a regular dream. Well, it was at first. But then every time I fell asleep, there was another one! And they kept getting more vivid, more *real*. Barbara Anne, it was like Edgar and I . . ."

"What?"

Henry swallowed hard. "It was as if Edgar and I had traded places somehow. And Edgar's world was the real one now. And I was just . . . an intruder."

Then Henry started to paint me a picture with his words. He said he dreamt that Edgar was there in the room with him, getting dressed. He watched as Edgar tied his shoes.

"They were weird shoes too, more like brown ice skates without the blades than regular shoes," Henry said.

As Edgar finished lacing up the tops, he called, "Mother! I'm ready to go."

Henry said he glanced toward the doorway, and he saw a woman there. The one who smelled like lilacs. The one who'd worn a mask in his other dream.

"Oh, Edgar," she said. "I'm afraid I have bad news. No cinema tonight. Father says they've closed them all. Just to be safe."

"Not really!" Edgar protested.

"It seems so," she said. "I'm sorry, dear, but this flu is serious business. I suppose the schools will be next."

Henry saw Edgar take off his tie and pull a wooden yo-yo out of his pocket. He wove the string through his fingers, until the yo-yo hung there in the center, swaying.

Henry paused then and said, "Don't just stare at me, Barbara Anne. Say something. Am I going crazy?"

"What?" I asked. "No!"

"Good," Henry said. He nodded like we'd agreed on something, like we'd made a pact. And then he told me the next part.

"The thing was that I kept trying to wake up, but I

couldn't seem to stay awake for very long. It was sort of like swimming in a lake, like I was pushing off against that soft bottom each time and trying to find the surface. But I never knew who would be there—I mean, which family—when I came up for air."

Henry said that he had this uneasy feeling that he wasn't where he belonged. He kept worrying that he was late for school. And then he heard this loud noise—not that obnoxious buzz of the tardy bell, though.

"This was something else," Henry said. "More like . . . church bells. Tolling."

Henry told me that he went to the window and looked out in time to see the strangest thing: an old-fashioned black carriage coming down the street, drawn by huge, dark horses.

"Every horse had a feather on its head. Just one. And they walked really slowly and so tall and straight, almost like acrobats in a circus ring. Do you know what I mean?"

I nodded so he would continue.

"The man who held the reins was dressed in a black top hat and cape," Henry said. "He turned his head and stared at me when he passed. And the carriage pulled this curtained glass box with another box inside. Except it wasn't just a box, Barbara Anne. It was a coffin."

CHAPTER NINETEEN

THE SMUDGE STICK

Henry and I had been sitting together on the front steps while he told me this story. And it was too cold to be outside. We could see our breath as we spoke. But after what Henry had described, I wasn't looking for an invitation to come for a visit, and I guess Henry was in no hurry to go back in either. So we just sat there, side by side, for a while.

Finally I said, "You know, she's lived in that house forever. Miss Leary. Since she and Edgar were little kids."

"How do you know?" Henry asked.

Then I explained about my visit on Thanksgiving, about how Edgar and Constance were childhood friends. "Like us," I said. "Best friends like us."

"I guess," Henry said. "If you were a strange old lady and I were a ghost."

"She made him sound so great," I said.

"For her, maybe," Henry said. "I just want him to go, Barbara Anne. I can't take it anymore. He has to leave."

"I know," I said. "We'll make him go. I promise, Henry."

I wasn't sure, at first, how I would keep my promise to Henry. A few days later, though, I got an idea. I came up with it because Renee was hopeless at fractions.

Zack was trying to help her with them. She seemed more willing to take his help than to ask me or Henry. Zack had trouble with reading, but he was pretty good at math.

"Look," Zack said. "If I had a pizza—"

"You'd eat the whole thing," Henry said.

"Stick a sock in it!" Zack said. "I'm trying to help her."

I thought he and Henry would get into it then. I expected a bunch of insults that would make Zack start doing his counting thing. But it didn't happen that way. Zack just gave Henry a look and then went back to helping Renee. He was pretty patient about it too.

"How's it going, Renee?" Ms. Biniam asked when she stopped by our pod.

"It's okay," Renee said. "I was having trouble, but Zack explained it to me."

"Renee," I heard Ms. Biniam say. "If you need help, all you have to do is ask."

That was it. I did some research, and the next day at lunch I said to Henry, "I think I know what to do. To get rid of Edgar. We need to ask him to leave."

"Great idea, Barbara Anne. I'll get going on a letter right away."

"No. Really. We need to just straight-out tell him that it's time to go. I've done some reading, and I have a whole list of what we need."

"Let me see that," Henry said, grabbing for my notebook.

For someone who didn't think it would work, he sure seemed curious about my plan. He opened the notebook to the first page and found this list:

1. Smudge stick
2. Bells
3. Casting a circle

"Smudge stick?" Henry asked.

"Yes," I told him. "Everybody does it. It's a bundle of herbs—sage mostly—and you set it on fire and wave it around. The smoke removes the spirits. It cleanses the space."

"Smoke?" Henry asked.

"Yeah," I said. "I know it seems drastic, but it's a time-honored method. I promise."

"For setting off smoke detectors," Henry said.

"We could always take the batteries out before we start," I said. "What? My grandmother does it all the time when she's cooking and something starts to burn. You just put them back in later."

"Look," Henry said. "We've done enough damage at my house already. If you don't mind, I'd rather not burn it to the ground."

"Okay, okay," I said. "So we'll just do the other two."

We agreed to go to his house after school the following day to test out methods two and three. Henry wasn't convinced they would work, but he didn't have anything to lose either.

"What are we waiting for?" Henry asked as we stood outside school the next day.

"Renee and Zack," I said.

"I thought it was just us."

"That won't work," I told him. "You can't cast a circle with two people."

"Oh, of course," Henry said. "What was I thinking?"

"Henry, you don't have to be so sarcastic. I'm trying to help."

"What's in there?" he asked, nodding toward the extra bag I was carrying.

"Tools of the trade," I said.

"You're really enjoying this, aren't you?" he asked.

I shrugged like it was no big deal, but we both knew what the answer was. Who doesn't want to test stuff out once they learn something new? And this wasn't something ordinary like making soup or finger knitting. (Although, I will say that there are some kids at school who can finger knit so quickly it's like a magic trick, and they have a strand now that stretches practically halfway across the playground—which is impressive, but still nothing compared to learning to banish a ghost.)

Zack and Renee joined us a couple of minutes later, and Zack couldn't wait to get started. "So, what do we have to do?" he asked. "Once we get there?"

"Oh, don't worry," Henry said. "Barbara Anne will tell us exactly what to do from now on."

I scowled at him, even though he was right, and the other two might as well know what they were in for. Some people just don't appreciate leadership ability.

When we got to Henry's room, I unpacked my canvas bag first thing. Here is what was inside:

- A candle
- Two bells
- A notebook and pen
- A small bunch of herbs tied with a string

"Is that a smudge stick?" Henry asked me. "I thought we said no smudge stick."

"Dude, relax," Zack said. "It's a tiny pile of leaves."

"He's right," I said. "Relax. Nobody's going to burn the house down. I'll be really careful. Besides, if it gets too smoky, I can switch to this."

I pulled one last thing from the bag: another candle. "Electric," I said.

"Hey, these are cute," Renee said, picking up one of the little bells. "Where'd you get them?"

"Leftovers from when my mom planned her friend's wedding reception," I said.

"Huh. What are they for?"

"Haven't you ever seen these? You ring them to make the bride and groom kiss." Then I added, "But we're not going to use them that way here. Obviously." Because I didn't think there was anything going on between Zack and Renee, but I didn't feel like testing it out.

"Okay," I said. "Let's start."

I had everybody stand in a circle and hold hands. I had Henry's hand on one side and Zack's on the other, and they both felt disgustingly moist. I didn't even want to think about how long it had been since Zack had washed his.

"Okay," I said. "Now take a giant step backward, but try to maintain the circle." I was using my most confident voice, because I learned at babysitter training that children will listen to you if you stay calm and sound sure of yourself. So far, it was working, even on Zack, and that was saying something.

Then I stepped out of position, lit the smudge stick, and walked toward the three of them, one at a time. At each side of the room, I waved the flaming herb bundle in a little circle. I was holding it up as high as I could—Statue of Liberty style—to make up for the fact that I'm not very tall. At each spot, I stopped and recited the words I'd memorized from the book.

Oh, great guardians of the north—

"I'm pretty sure that's the south," Henry said.
Renee shushed him.
"I'm just saying."
But it was ruined then, so I had to start over.

Oh, great guardians of the south
Cleanse this space and
Protect all those who reside within!

The smoke was beginning to get kind of thick, which was really not my fault but more a result of the way everybody kept interrupting me. That and, I guess, the fact that we forgot to open a window before we started.

Renee kept coughing.

"Finish up before she hacks up a lung," Zack said.

"Okay, okay!"

We cast out all who are
Unwelcome
Let them now depart!

Everything got quiet then, and that's when we all heard it: the creak of the stairs, the sound of someone—or something—slowly approaching. Then, of course, Renee screamed, a sound so high and shrill that dogs should have been the only ones able to hear it. And then, through the toxic smudge-stick haze, Alice materialized in the doorway in her leotard, her hands on her hips. She did not look happy.

"You forgot to pick me up from dance class!" she yelled at Henry. "You were supposed to walk me home."

The way she looked at the four of us destroyed the whole thing. Suddenly it seemed ridiculous.

Alice waved one hand through the toxic air and said, "Are you guys *smoking*?! 'Cause if you are, I'm telling."

"Of course we're not smoking," Henry said.

"It's Barbara Anne's fault," Zack said. "For burning that smidgen wand."

He had a point. I was having trouble putting it out too. I blew on it, but that just seemed to keep it going. "Renee!" I yelled. "Open the window!" I felt like a runner in some crazy relay race where nobody would take the baton.

"Open it! Open it!" I yelled at Renee. Boy, she really was not good in an emergency.

"You are in so much trouble," Alice said to Henry as the smoke detectors began to beep.

"Have you got a fire extinguisher?" Zack asked her.

"I don't know!" Alice said.

Finally Renee got the window open, and I pushed the smudge stick through it.

"Why are you giving it more air?" Henry yelled. "Do you not understand anything about fire?"

He ran over and tried to grab it out of my hand, and in the struggle, the smudge stick dropped out of the window and landed on Henry's front lawn.

This was the bad news.

The good news, I guess, was that Sophie had just gotten

home, and she doused it with that giant water bottle she always carries. (She likes to stay well hydrated.)

I watched the last of the smoke from the smudge stick drift up to where Henry and I were hanging out of the window. I didn't know what to do, so I waved. "Hi, Sophie," I said. "Welcome home."

CHAPTER TWENTY

THE HOSPITAL

Explaining the whole smudge-stick thing would not have been easy. I guess I was lucky that Sophie didn't even ask. She just kept opening windows and told Zack, Renee, and me that it was time to go home. When I tried to say something, she pushed her palm toward me, which is pretty much the international sign for *I don't want to hear it!* My dad wanted to know, though, so I had to tell him that we lit a candle and it fell over. Fortunately, he launched into a long lecture about fire safety, and by the time it ended, he didn't even think to ask why we needed a candle at four in the afternoon. Also, he said those magic words: "Let's not mention this to your mother."

Not long after that, though, I had a real problem because

Henry got sick again. Really sick. I was afraid that maybe it was all the smoke from the smudge stick, but my dad said that had nothing to do with it. He told me that it's caused by either a virus or bacteria, depending on what kind you have. Pneumonia. That's what Henry had. And, for obvious reasons, the sound of that word terrified me. As soon as I found out, I wanted to go and check on him, but apparently hospitals have some ridiculous rule about how old you have to be to visit—which is why we had to sneak in instead of just going there like regular people, which, by the way, children are.

Zack understood right away that we should go and make sure that Henry was all right, but Renee put up a fuss as soon as I mentioned it.

"Oh, no," she said. "I do NOT do hospitals. I can't even stand the smell. Besides, you're gonna get in trouble, Barbara Anne. We all are."

I would have argued with her, but she sounded serious. And I could see how Renee might be scared; it was probably because of her mom. So I turned to Zack.

"Where is he?" Zack asked.

"Pacific Lutheran," I said.

"Oh, great," Zack said.

"What?"

"That's where my mom works."

"That's perfect," I said. But Zack wasn't so sure.

In the end, though, he went along with me. Who knows why? Like my grandmother says, "People are complicated." Zack took a chance. He helped me get to Henry when nobody else would.

When Zack and I decided to visit Henry, I was part excited, part scared. In my daydream, I pictured escaping from my bedroom in the moonlight—out the window, hand over hand, using a ladder that I'd made myself from bedsheets. (This was never very realistic because I still hated the new gym teacher and had not been persuaded to "work" on my upper body strength.) Imagine my disappointment, though, when I was able to walk right out of the house after dinner without anybody even noticing.

My dad went into his office to work on his computer, and my mom was getting Rachel ready for her bath.

"Well," I said. "I have a lot of homework, so I guess I'll just get to it."

"Okay," my mom said. "Sounds good."

You'd think she would have had a few questions, but no! Not this time! She just closed the bathroom door—right in my face! I was one hundred percent sure that she had not heard a word I said. I could have told her, "By the way, Mom, there's a sea monster in Green Lake, and I spotted him on my walk home." Or, "Gee, Mom, you don't mind if I grab your keys and teach myself to drive now, do you?" And she would have had that same answer: "Okay. Sounds good."

I have heard of people, people with observant parents, I suppose, who have to come up with all sorts of cover stories and excuses. (I had a few ready.) There are people, I am told, who even leave a note behind to misdirect anybody who might be looking for them. (I had one written and ready to go.) But there was no need. Nobody cared where I was or what I was up to. No reason to tiptoe room to room, eyes darting around like a cartoon cat burglar. I just strolled out and walked over to Zack's house. Hiding all those pillows under the blankets in the shape of my body had been a big waste of time.

I could see Zack through the front window when I got there. He was sitting at the dining room table with an older kid, like high school age, and he looked really cute. Not Zack. The other one. He had wavy brown hair that was just a little bit long, sort of Disney prince length. Not that I cared. I'm just reporting the facts. Who cared, really, what he looked like? But also, why was he there, and how would I get Zack out of the house now? It was the first interesting difficulty—the first step on my quest to get to Henry. And I had an idea. I saw some tiny stones on the ground near the door, so I grabbed a handful and tossed them at the window.

Then I ducked behind a bush. I was pretty proud of myself until Zack answered the door.

"Barbara Anne!" he hollered. "We can see you!"

This forced me out from behind the bush, so he did not need to continue, but he decided to anyway. "Why don't you just ring the bell like a normal person?" he asked.

"Well, I . . ."

"Oh, never mind," Zack said. "Just come on in."

He motioned toward an empty chair at the dining room table. They were eating sandwiches.

"This is Doug," he said.

"Aren't you going to offer her a sandwich?" Doug asked.

"Dude, you're not my mother," Zack said.

"Hi," I said. "I'm Barbara Anne. Klein. I'm Zack's—"

"She sits across from me," Zack said. "At school."

"Good to meet you," Doug said. "I live across from him. Used to be his babysitter before he got so polite and mature." He smiled, and I noticed that he had very blue eyes and long eyelashes. "I should go," he said to Zack. "Behave yourself. Nice to meet you, Barbara Anne."

After he left, Zack said, "You can stop staring at the door, Barbara Anne. He's not going to reappear."

"I was not staring at the door!" I said. But I was. I totally was.

"He's a pretty nice guy," Zack said.

"How long have you known him?"

"Since third grade. He was the only one my mom could get to babysit me when I was in my 'acting out' phase."

"What's that?"

Zack shrugged and kept chewing on his sandwich. "I don't know. That's what my counselor called it. My parents weren't getting along with each other, and I wasn't getting along with anybody!" Zack laughed.

"That's not funny!" I said.

"No," Zack said. "It really wasn't. I used to break stuff. Major temper tantrums. But, you know. My parents settled down, and so did I. So now Doug and me are just neighbors."

I was sort of surprised, almost impressed, that Zack told me all that. I would have asked him more, but the doorbell rang. Zack hopped up to get it, and there was Renee. I looked out the window and saw her father waving goodbye from behind the wheel of his car.

"I thought you didn't want to come," I said to Renee.

"If you're worried about Henry, then so am I," she said.

"Enough jibber-jab," Zack said. "It's getting late."

"Jibber-jab?" I asked, but Zack just ignored me. He wrote out a note to his mom, left it on the table, and started talking about what bus we had to take.

You would think that if we were going to get lost, it would be because we took the wrong bus, got off at the wrong stop, or made a wrong turn on the way to the hospital. But none of that happened. We found our way to the hospital like we'd been going there every day of our lives. Once we got inside, though, it was a different story. We went through the big lobby toward the elevators, and then I looked at Zack.

"Now what?" I asked. "Which way do we go?"

It was clear from the look on his face that he had no idea.

"You're kidding me!" I said. "Didn't your mom ever take you around? Give you a tour? Introduce you to people?"

I was thinking of the time my dad took me to his office on Take Our Kids to Work Day. Maybe it was different, though, if your parents were doctors. I guess you wouldn't just get to hang around gawking in the middle of somebody's operation. What are your parents going to say? "Hi, this is my younger son, Jimmy. He'll be handing me my scalpels today"? I don't think so. Still, this was a setback.

"Pick a floor and get in," I said, because standing in front of the elevator like a litter of lost puppies seemed like the surest way to draw attention to ourselves.

So we started. There were signs, kind of a lot of them, but they were confusing, and the hallway was just blank white walls, more elevators, and strange doors with high, small windows. There were labs, miniature gated-off coffee shops, a gift shop with scarves and a teapot in the window. The place was huge. More like a small city than a building. It was already starting to seem that we might be here all night, wandering around like mice in a maze.

"I don't like it here," Renee said.

"We just got started!" I yelled.

I know. I should have been more sympathetic. I could have offered to help her find her way back to the lobby and told her to wait there. I could have told her that it would be okay, or maybe even promised that we would leave soon. But I didn't do any of that because I was too mad. It was infuriating how easily she was willing to give up.

"Don't be such a baby, Renee!"

"But this place is creepy," she said.

Zack was ignoring us both. "Let's try the next floor," he said.

And so we did.

Things were even worse on the next floor, because instead of lots of emptyish hallways, we finally found the rooms. That was progress, I guess, but peeking into them was awful. The rooms were mostly white with curtains hanging down the center, and there was lots of coughing and machines beeping and sometimes someone moaning. Also, there was the sound of sniffling, which was my fault because it was coming from Renee, and I was the one who had made her cry.

"Are you guys lost?" a nurse asked us.

"Oh, no," I said. "She's just upset because our grandmother is leaving. Dying. I mean, we were just leaving."

"Really," she said.

She wasn't stupid. We ran toward the elevators.

"This isn't working," Zack said. "Let's just go."

"One more floor," I said. "Please! We came all this way."

And on the next floor, my persistence paid off. We found Henry. We found him because I would not give up and because Henry would not eat orange Jell-O. His half-eaten tray was outside in the hallway, and I saw the little card with the number and his name:

322, Bed A
Davis, Henry

And then I saw something else: an exact rerun of Henry's dream about Edgar's mother. In the dim light of Henry's hospital room, a woman was perched on the edge of the bed. She wore a white blouse and a longish skirt. Her hand was outstretched; she was running her fingers gently through Henry's hair. Then she turned her head and looked at me, and I could see that the lower half of her face was covered by a surgical mask, just as Henry had described. She rose and walked toward me.

I screamed, and I'm not even ashamed. It was a big scream too. A real shriek. It lasted a couple of long seconds. It went on the whole while that she got up and crossed the room. It lasted until I ran out of breath, really, which was almost exactly the same moment that I realized she was solid and real.

By then, I had drawn a crowd: Renee and Zack plus a couple of nurses, all looking petrified.

The woman reached me, lowered her mask, and extended her hand. "I'm sorry I startled you," she said.

"It's okay," Renee answered for me. "She's always like this."

The woman laughed. "I'm Christine," she said. "Henry's mother. And you must be the famous Barbara Anne."

I shook her hand. Over her shoulder I could see that Henry's eyes were open. He was alive and smiling.

CHAPTER TWENTY-ONE

A TURN FOR THE WORSE

Sneaking back into the house that night was not nearly as easy as getting out had been. My mother was still up when I went through the back door, key in hand. We faced off in the center of the checkerboard tile of the kitchen floor like square-dance partners about to do-si-do. She did not look happy. She had been doing the dishes, and now she stood with her hands on her hips, scowling. Tiny soap bubbles were still melting away on her fingers.

"Just exactly where did you come from?" she wanted to know.

The exact answer? That was room 322, bed A, but I was certain that was not what she would want to hear. Now, I realize adults stress telling the truth, but in the end, aren't there always times when they'd be better off not knowing it? Maybe not. But you should have seen the look on her face. It was scary. I panicked.

"I thought I heard something," I said. "A noise. Outside. Yes. A loud noise. Outside the house. This house. Our house."

Why could I not shut up? Her eyes were like lightsabers that had just clicked on; she tried to sound calm, but I could tell she was ready to do battle.

"Really?" she said.

"Uh-huh."

Faced with her silence, I was forced to go on. "And you'll be glad to know that the whole yard is empty. Yep. Empty. No bears or burglars or anything. So we're good here. Safe."

She said nothing. Just kept staring the death stare.

"So . . . you're welcome," I said. "And . . ."

Stay strong! I was telling myself. *Stay strong! Don't crack! Think of something!*

"I'll just be going back to bed," I said.

"Sleeping in your jeans these days, are you?"

"Well, no," I said, trying to laugh, but my voice was beginning to crack. "This is just—obviously . . . you know, you don't want to be facing a bear, potentially, in pajamas."

"No," my mom said. "I'd have to agree with you there, Barbara Anne. Nothing more terrifying than a bear in pajamas."

"Hah! Good one, Mom. I—"

"I have no idea where you've been, young lady. Or what you've been up to, but I do know that you will not be leaving this house unescorted or going anywhere besides school for the rest of the month. I'll take care of any bears that might wander by."

"Or burglars," I said. "It could easily have been—"

"Barbara Anne!"

"Right," I said.

But what if I actually had been trying to save her? So ungrateful, really.

I had trouble falling asleep that night. I was mad at my mom, first of all. And disappointed that I hadn't really gotten to spend any time with Henry. And every time I started to fall asleep, I'd feel this small, funny bit of guilt about leaving Henry there in the hospital. I knew they would take care of him. I knew his family was there. It was just that he'd looked so—well—*little* in that bed. And I couldn't imagine what it would be like spending the whole night in some strange place, with hundreds of rooms—being just a number. I hoped they cared about him. Henry. I hoped they understood who he was, what he meant to all of us outside, in the real world.

Sometimes, when my dad's on a business trip, I make

him hold the phone up to show me the room. It always looks the same; it's just a desk and a bed and a TV. But somehow I feel better, seeing the whole room and not just his face floating inside my mom's cell phone screen. It was like that with Henry too. Seeing him made me feel a little better, but I still wanted him out of that place, where every room looked the same. I wanted him home.

In my dreams that night, I was at school—a version of school that I couldn't recognize. The playground had changed. The play structures were much taller, with no wood chips below to break your fall. They looked like something that only an acrobat could manage. The sky was growing dark. A storm was coming. The playground was empty. And I stood at the school door, pulling as hard as I could, trying to get it to open.

I heard a boy's voice call to me. "It's locked," he said. "Closed."

I turned to see who was there but discovered I was still alone. I kept struggling with the door, desperate to get in. Huge gusts of wind pushed against me. Then, somehow, through the roar, I heard two words. "Find Henry." I turned back to ask why, to see who was there with me. Nothing. No one. Crows lined the metal bars. They screeched at me and flew away. Black wings scattering across the darkening sky.

My grandmother was there, at the edge of my bed, when I opened my eyes. It was morning. "Bitsy," she said. "Wake up. You're having a bad dream."

I wrapped my arms around her. She felt so solid, and warm, and real. Everything seemed okay for a minute, until I remembered that Henry was sick and I was grounded.

"Where's my mom?" I asked. I figured I couldn't start too soon on getting back on her good side.

"She's taking your dad to the airport," my grandmother said. "Work trip."

And so my grandmother fixed me breakfast and walked me to school with Rachel in the stroller. It was cold but sunny, and it felt good to have the air hit my face, to take my place in our pod of desks and listen to Ms. Biniam describe the day ahead. It felt normal. Present tense. Except for Henry's empty desk, everything was just the way it was supposed to be. I wish it had lasted.

My grandmother picked me up from school too, and I knew as soon as I saw her that something was wrong. She likes to say that she's an "open book," which means she doesn't bother to keep secrets. And when she's upset, you can tell right away.

"What happened?" I asked her.

"Would you like some ice cream?" she asked.

"It's freezing out," I said. "Who wants ice cream? I just want to know what's wrong."

A man behind us, who was putting out Christmas decorations, turned for a second to stare. I guess my voice was getting too loud. My grandmother patted my mittened hand and pulled me along.

"There's been a little development," she said. "It's Henry. They've moved him, honey—to the ICU."

"I want to go and see him," I said. "I didn't really get to talk to him last night. I—"

"I'm sorry, Bitsy. You can't."

"I'm eleven," I said. "That's only one year off from their stupid rule."

"It isn't that," she said. "He's in a special section. Family only. No matter how old you are."

"But I am his family," I told her.

I refused to eat dinner that night, partly because it was meat loaf, but mostly because I was worried about Henry.

"I know I'm grounded," I told my mom. "But you could make an exception this one time!"

"Honey, I would let you go if I could. But I don't make the rules," she said.

And that really scared me because, of course, she did

make the rules in my world. I knew there were things she couldn't control. I just didn't like to think about it.

"Couldn't I just go there and ask them how he is? The nurses there are really nice."

I had no idea, by the way, if this was true. All I'd done so far was run from them and terrify them by screaming.

"Try not to worry," my mom said. "His parents are there, and everyone is taking good care of him, Barbara Anne."

"His mother came all the way from England to make sure he'd be okay," my grandmother added.

They were talking over my head now, and I hate that. All I got to do was watch and listen and turn my head from one to the other like I was watching a tennis match.

"I'm relieved she's here," my grandmother said. "I have a bad feeling about this."

"Mom!" my mom said, and she looked down at me.

"Oh, right, sorry. Bitsy, why don't you go see what's on television?"

I went in the other room and turned on the set, but of course I didn't bother to watch it, not when the real story was unfolding in the kitchen. I tiptoed toward the doorway so that I could hear the rest of their conversation.

"You don't have to go," I heard my grandmother say. "You stay here with Rachel. I'll take her."

"I don't think we should intrude," my mom said.

"We'll stay in the waiting room," my grandmother said. "It'll make her feel better."

I'm not sure what made my mom say yes. Maybe it was because my grandmother's my mom's mom, and no matter how old you get, sometimes your mom is still the boss of you.

"Go get your shoes, Barbara Anne," my grandmother said. She didn't say it loudly either. I think she knew I'd been right there listening the whole time.

I was so relieved that I would get to go and check on Henry. I threw my arms around my grandmother. "Thank you," I told her.

The waiting room was plain and ugly. It had plastic orange chairs that were hard to get comfortable in. Henry's dad was there, but he was mostly pacing back and forth a little way down the hall and talking on his cell phone. I couldn't hear much of what he said, but sometimes I would catch a word or two. And so far, my least favorite were "heart monitor."

Then I heard the ding of the elevator, and I saw Uncle Marty get off. He looked older than he had at the library. His hair was messed up, and his eyes looked sleepy. I pointed him out to my grandmother. "That's Henry's uncle Marty," I said.

"Do you want to go and say hello?" she asked.

I nodded and walked over. "Barbara Anne," he said. "I'm surprised to see you here so late."

"My grandmother brought me," I said.

Then Christine, Henry's mom, came out. She gave Uncle Marty a hug and didn't let go. She said something to him too, but I couldn't understand what it was. Her voice was all funny and muffled. "When's the last time you had anything to eat?" he asked her.

She shrugged and then came over to us to thank us for checking in on Henry. "I think we're going down to the cafeteria before it closes," she said. "Can I bring you anything?"

"No, thank you," my grandmother said. "Just take care of yourself."

Then the elevator was there, and Christine and Uncle Marty were gone. Henry's dad came over and said to us what he'd said on the phone. "They've got him on a heart monitor. They're worried about arrhythmia." He looked at me and said, "That's an irregular heartbeat. But he's going to be okay. Maybe you should go home and get some rest. You've got school in the morning."

I begged my grandmother to stay just a little longer, so we did. And she was the one who got some rest. She fell completely asleep in her chair, head tilted toward the side, mouth open. And that's when it happened.

The waiting room was empty and quiet—except for a soft snore from my grandmother. The sound from the television was turned down low, and there was only the light from the screen and one little lamp burning dimly in the corner. I think I was starting to fall asleep myself, but I know what happened.

The room felt a bit colder, and I shivered. Then I heard the voice from my dream, and suddenly I knew the breathy whisper in my ear was Edgar. "Find Henry," he said. "Push the button!"

I jumped up from my chair and raced through the swinging doors. I was running down the narrow hallway, frantic. I followed the signs for the Intensive Care Unit. And when I arrived, my heart still pounding, everything shifted. The room was dimly lit and completely silent. I looked over at Henry. His eyes were closed, and his face was as pale as the sheets, but he seemed to be sleeping. Peacefully. I felt foolish then. Maybe I'd been dreaming; maybe I'd only thought I heard Edgar.

Then his voice became more urgent. "Press the button!"

"Where?" I said out loud.

Then, above Henry's head, I saw it. I reached over him, leaned in, and pushed. It seemed like forever, but it was only seconds before the nurse came into Henry's room.

"Did you use the call button?" she asked. She did not look happy.

"You need to check on my friend," I said.

"We are," she told me. "He's being continuously monitored and—"

Before she could finish her sentence, the beeping started. I stared at the red jagged line on the little screen next to Henry's bed, wishing I could understand it. Then I looked at Henry. His eyes were open now, and he looked terrified.

"You have to go," the nurse said. "You can't be in here."

And the others came then, pushing past me into the room, heading toward Henry. I don't know how things would have worked out if Edgar hadn't whispered to me. I suppose they would have reached Henry fast enough. I hope they would have. All I know is that Edgar was there when Henry needed him, and because of Edgar, so was I.

CHAPTER TWENTY-TWO

FORTUNES AND FAREWELLS

Of course, I was not the only one who had been worrying about Henry. Once they knew I had been to see him, Zack and Renee wanted a full update. And Zack didn't wait either. He started asking a bunch of questions the next day at school. Right in the middle of silent reading.

"So, is he going to die?" Zack asked.

"Zack!" Renee said.

"What? That's what we all want to know, isn't it?"

"How is Barbara Anne supposed to know? She isn't a doctor."

"She went to see him," Zack said.

"I think he'll be fine," I said. I couldn't explain how I

knew. I had decided not to tell them—or anyone—about Edgar, about how he helped me, about what he did for Henry. "I'm going to see Constance," I said. "She'll know."

"How will *she* know?" Zack demanded.

"She'll tell my fortune," I explained. "She'll see it—in the cards."

"Table three!" Ms. Biniam said. "A little less conversation, please. This is *silent* reading time."

I guess I was still technically grounded, but on the days my grandmother watched me, I could get away with pretty much anything, and even my mom didn't remember to enforce it all the time. That morning, when I told my mom I planned to visit Miss Leary after school, all she said was, "That's a sweet idea, Bitsy. I'll pick you up as soon as I'm done shopping."

And Constance might have been surprised when I turned up on her doorstep, but she seemed happy to see me.

"How's your little friend?" she asked. "How's Henry? We've been so worried."

"How do you know about Henry?" I asked her.

"He was mentioned," she said. "At church."

"I think he's going to be okay. I hope he will be. My mom told me he's not in intensive care anymore. But that's partly why I came," I said. "I thought maybe you would know."

Constance looked at me, puzzled, until I went on. "Can you tell my fortune?" I asked her.

"Of course," she said. "Let's get out the cards."

Constance and I settled ourselves in the living room, and she asked her helper to make some tea. Then she dealt out the cards with her crooked fingers and began. "Let's see what we have," she said. Of course she gave me only good news. And some of it might have been made up. I mean, who ever heard of a fortune-teller reminding you to study and do all your homework? But she wasn't telling me what I wanted to know most, and so I had to ask.

"What about Henry?" I asked. "He'll be all right, won't he?"

Her expression changed, and she looked more serious.

"Barbara Anne," she said gently. "Nobody knows the future. I wish I could tell you what lies ahead, but I can't. I can only say that whatever it is, happy or sad, you won't be in it alone. You have family and good friends."

"I know," I said. "But Henry is my only close friend."

"Oh, I'm sure that's not true," she said. "And even if it were, he's taught you, already, how to make others. That's what our friends do for us."

"Did Edgar do that?" I asked. "For you?"

Constance nodded.

"You must miss him," I said.

"I do," she told me. "But he's with me still. I like to think of Edgar as my guardian angel."

"I think he's Henry's too," I said.

"Well," she told me. "I guess I don't mind sharing."

I offered to carry her teacup to the kitchen, and when I got back, I saw that Constance had closed her eyes. At first, I thought she was just resting for a minute, but it went on too long. I knew she must be asleep or . . . I leaned across the table and stared at her as hard as I could in the dim light. I held my own breath until I saw her chest was moving. Then I got up and headed to the door. Miss Leary's helper stepped out into the hallway.

"She fell asleep," I said. "Will you tell her I said goodbye?"

"Of course," she said. "She's asleep more often than not these days."

My jacket was hanging on a hook in the hallway. And as I reached for it, I saw a photo I had never noticed before. It was a picture of Edgar and a girl with dark, curly hair, a girl who looked a little . . . like me.

"Beautiful children, weren't they?" Miss Leary's helper asked. "It's hard to believe Constance was ever that young. And the boy was so talented. A prodigy on the piano. Such a shame. You're a dear to visit her. I hope we see you again soon."

I told her I would be back soon, though I had no idea if it was true. Then I took my jacket and stood outside on the porch, waiting for my mother. The lights were on in Henry's house, and I could see Sophie in the window watering a plant. It looked so cozy, and I wished more than anything that I could ring the bell, that Henry would be there to open the door and welcome me.

At school the next day, we were scheduled to share our artifact reports, and it was Renee's turn. She stood in front of the class, looking straight down at her paper. Her voice was soft and a little shaky. "When most people think of Thomas Edison, they think of this," she said, and she held up a lightbulb. "Or they remember that he created the phonograph and the first motion pictures. He was a brilliant man. People called him the Wizard of Menlo Park, and he had more than a thousand patents for inventions."

I was sleepy and still worried about Henry, and I'll admit that I wasn't listening too closely. I guess I expected it to be the usual stuff. You know, when he was born and when he died and a long, dull list of everything he invented. But then Renee started talking about something I'd never heard of before: a spirit phone.

"The spirit phone, or spirit box, may have been the last invention that Edison worked on," Renee said. "And nobody knows if he ever finished it or even if he left behind draw-ings. Some people said that it was just a joke that Edison was playing and not even a real thing."

Renee stopped for a minute then and looked out ner-vously at the class.

"Go on," Ms. Biniam said. "Tell us more, Renee."

Renee went on, but she wasn't even looking at her paper anymore. She was just talking to all of us. "Well," she said. "It was right after World War One, and a lot of people died in that war. So people were interested in finding ways to communicate with the people they had lost. And Edison, he was a scientist, so he didn't believe in most of the things that they were doing, like séances and mediums who try to talk to the dead. But he did think that maybe some part of us, our personalities, I guess, might go on. So some people say that he was building a machine, the last and greatest machine of his career, to record . . . the voices of ghosts."

"What do you think, Renee?" Ms. Biniam asked.

"Well, I'm not sure," Renee said. "But there was this guy, this journalist in France, and he says he found a section of Edison's diary that nobody else had ever seen. And it was all about finding ways to reconnect with people who have died. And I think he could have done it, maybe, if he'd had more time. Because sometimes it does seem like the past isn't really over and done with. And everyone would have been rooting for him, to find a way, you know, to deliver those messages to the people who needed them. And that way people could have something besides just memories."

There was so much feeling in her voice. I could hear it gathering as each word joined the next. It was like watching raindrops slide down a window, merge, and fall.

When she finished and took her seat, Ms. Biniam said quietly, "Thank you, Renee."

When school was ending the next day, Ms. Biniam said, "I have a special project, and I need a volunteer."

I barely heard her. I wasn't really paying attention. I was stuffing a worksheet inside my backpack and wondering if we would keep getting this much homework right through winter break. Probably we would. Biniam was relentless. She was also staring right at me.

"Barbara Anne?" she asked. "Wouldn't you like to volunteer?"

"For what?" I asked.

"The army," Zack said, and then laughed alone at his own joke.

"To make a special delivery," she said. "Henry needs his homework, and I thought you might like to bring it to him."

"You're making him do homework in the hospital?" I asked.

"Of course not," she said. "He was discharged. This morning."

Biniam was smiling. I nearly started to cry.

I was so happy to see Henry that I really didn't want to even think about anything that came before. Still, a part of me was curious too. I had to know—how it was for him.

"Do you remember it?" I asked him. "Any of it?"

"Not really," he said. "I was dreaming."

And then he told me—one last time—about *them*.

In the dream, it seemed to Henry that his mother was with him, sitting on the edge of the bed. She faced away from him, with her hands covering her face. She was crying. Henry said that he tried to ask her what was wrong, but she didn't seem to be able to hear him. And when he tried to sit up, to put his arm around her, Henry realized that he couldn't move. This strange, sudden paralysis scared Henry more than his mother's tears. He didn't understand why his body had stopped working. But it had. He was pinned down to the bed as if someone were holding him there. All he could do was listen to his mother sob and watch the strange, dark shadows pass across the ceiling.

"They looked like clouds," Henry said. "Like storm clouds forming."

Eventually, she stopped crying and turned toward him.

And that's when Henry realized his mistake. As she leaned forward to kiss his forehead, Henry saw that she wasn't his mother at all. And when her cold lips touched Henry's brow, she whispered her own son's name: "Edgar," she said.

She reached toward Henry's throat, and he tried to scream, but no sound came.

Gently, she adjusted something at his neck, tied a knot, and patted Henry's chest. Then the ghost rose up and unfolded a huge white sheet. It opened over Henry's head like a parachute and floated down softly, landing across his face and body, covering Henry in gauzy white from head to toe.

"He's ready now," Henry heard her say.

And his eyes flew open.

"And you were there," Henry said. "When the doctors came running in. How did you get there, Barbara Anne?"

I didn't know what else to say, so I told him the truth. "Edgar sent me," I answered.

"Edgar?" Henry asked, and so I nodded.

"You know," Henry said. "He was all I thought about while I was in the hospital. And being all cooped up in there alone . . . well, I think I finally understand him, Barbara Anne. It must have been so awful for him, trapped in that room, our room, all those days and nights. Maybe I never needed to be so afraid of him, you know? Maybe he just wanted what he asked for in the beginning, to have somebody to play with."

CHAPTER TWENTY-THREE

A DARK AND STORMY NIGHT

Everyone who knew Henry was so happy he had gotten better that we decided to celebrate. We would have had a welcome-home party for him, but Sophie was already planning a big surprise party for Constance, so the two things just got combined. Constance was turning 103! Sophie planned to send a picture to the newspaper and everything. For all we knew, Constance might be the oldest person in the world!

"What do you think we should get her?" I asked Henry as we walked home from school the day before the party.

"I have no idea," Henry said. "What could she possibly need that she doesn't already have?"

"Nothing," I said. "Which means you just get her

something she doesn't need. But something nice, like flowers or jewelry."

"Well," Henry said. "In that case, I might have one idea."

Henry's idea was that we should give Constance the locket from the trunk. And he could tell from the look on my face that I wasn't enthusiastic about that plan.

"Unless you think she'll be creeped out by it," Henry said. "Because it belonged to Edgar's mother, and she's, you know, dead."

"No," I said. "I think she'll like it."

"Great," Henry said. "Problem solved. You still have it, right? You didn't lose it or anything?"

"Have a little faith, Henry."

I still had it. I liked wearing it. And I hate to admit it, but I kind of wanted to keep it all for myself. But Constance was my friend now, and Edgar had been hers. I had told my mother that I didn't know who the locket belonged to, and I never changed my story, even after Constance told me that Edgar's mother had always worn it. But then, my mother didn't know anything about what we'd really been up to all these weeks since school started. Constance and Uncle Marty were the only grown-ups who knew—Marty because he studied history, and Constance because she had lived it.

So, later that afternoon, I polished the locket and took one last look at the faded picture of Edgar that was inside.

Then I put it in a little white box and asked my grandmother to tie a blue ribbon around it. She's the best at bows.

And, in the end, I was glad I let Henry have his way. For two reasons. The first was that Henry had been through a lot, with Edgar and all, and it seemed like he should be the one to make the decision this time. The other thing was that I kept thinking of Edgar, of the way he had missed Constance's birthday party long ago. It may sound strange, but it almost felt like bringing her the locket would be a way to bring Edgar to the party with us. I could hardly wait to see Constance's face when she opened it. Henry and I were both sure it would be the best gift she got.

Unfortunately, the night the party arrived, so did a huge storm. The wind was already blowing hard when my family and I got to Miss Leary's house. Sophie was afraid that the weather might spoil things, that people might not want to come. But everyone was there. Henry's mom and Uncle Marty arrived together, and they were soaked to the bone just getting from the car to the front door. Zack and Renee got a ride from Zack's mom, and Zack had his guitar with him. My whole family was there, of course. And Henry's was too. Everybody was talking about the rain, watching through the windows as it turned into a full-on thunderstorm. Lightning and everything.

Constance was the only one who didn't seem bothered by the weather. "I love a good storm," she said.

Rachel was less enthusiastic. She kept bursting into tears every time she heard the thunder. My grandmother said she was probably getting a new tooth, but I think she was afraid. She would not settle down. Maybe she was the first one to sense that something was off.

Uncle Marty and Henry's mom were sitting in one corner of the living room, talking about the research she had been doing in England. I had almost forgotten that Henry and I were not the only ones who had been studying up on ghosts.

"Your mom's project sounds great," I said.

"Yeah," Henry said. "At least her ghosts only exist in Shakespeare."

The lights flickered then, and my dad interrupted everyone to say, "I think we better get this show on the road before the electricity decides to go out."

The words were barely out of his mouth when the power failed, sending him scrambling for matches and candles. Constance seemed to have a million of them, and soon the whole place was glowing. There were a few flashlights too, and my dad let us have them.

"Hey," Zack said. "Let's play hide-and-seek."

Sophie didn't think that was such a great idea. After all, we were in someone else's house. But Constance said, "They won't hurt anything. Let them have fun."

"All right," Sophie said. "Can't argue with the guest of

honor. A quick game," she told us. "Just until we get the cake and coffee ready." My mother and Sophie returned to the kitchen, and Alice shouted, "Not it!"

Most of the house was pitch-black, and the rest was covered in eerie shadows because of the candlelight. Renee was it, so she got a flashlight, and everyone else hurried to hide ourselves in the darkness, behind doors and chairs. I could hear my dad dealing with Rachel, and my grandmother and Henry's dad talking to Constance. Farther away were the faint noises of Sophie and my mom putting the finishing touches on a cake that would probably set a world record for most candles.

"Ready or not, here I come!" Renee yelled to us.

My hiding spot was a far corner of the living room, where I wedged myself behind a chair next to one of the many bookcases. I crouched there in my stocking feet and felt something hard and round under my heel. A marble. Even in the dark, I could tell that much. Of course, I remembered the other time, when marbles bounced down the stairs toward me. This time, I wasn't scared. It was only one. Only one marble. It didn't necessarily mean that Edgar was here. And even if he were, the thought of him didn't scare me anymore. I picked it up and slipped it into my pocket. "Very funny, Edgar," I whispered. Then I felt a tap on my shoulder that made me gasp, and jump.

"I found you," Renee said. "You have to help me search

now." She was holding a flashlight under her chin, and it made her face look creepy. I let out a nervous laugh before I agreed to go with her.

The others were easy to find. I saw Zack's shoes sticking out from below the curtains in the dining room. Henry was behind the couch. And I heard Alice talking in the kitchen. She was eating icing off her finger. When I announced that I could see her, she just shrugged. "I don't care. I quit anyway."

"Let's play again," Zack said. "That was too easy. We should use the upstairs!"

"We can't do that," Renee said.

"Why not?"

"She's right, Zack. That's her private space," Henry said.

"What do you think is there, anyway?" Renee asked. She still had the flashlight in her hand, and now she was pointing it toward the staircase. There, on the bottom step, was a small card. Renee picked it up. It said:

A FRIEND WILL CALL FROM FAR AWAY.

"What is it?" Zack said.

"I think it's a card from the fortune-telling game," I said. I picked it up and put it in my pocket with the marble.

"Let me see," Renee said. But before I could show her, my mom called, "Kids! Come to the table!"

"Is it time for cake?" Zack asked.

"First we have to let Constance open her presents," my mom said.

Constance was at the head of the table with a pile of packages in front of her. She smiled as she watched us come into the room. It was strange. To see the house so full of people. It seemed so different from my other visits when I'd been alone, or with Henry. Constance must have felt it too.

"Thank you all for being here," she said. "The real gift of this evening is your friendship."

"Open ours first," I told Constance. "It's from Henry and me."

I watched as she undid the ribbon. "It's beautiful," she told us as soon as she saw the locket. Then she opened it, and smiled again. "How sweet to see this face today," she said. "To have him here."

"Who is it?" my father asked.

"A boy I knew," she said. "Long ago."

My mother was standing next to me, and she whispered, "Barbara Anne, that locket doesn't really belong to you."

"Trust me," I said. "She's the one who's supposed to have it now."

I picked up the locket to help Constance put it on. I couldn't believe my eyes. There was Edgar's photo—not the faded version that I had last seen, but one that looked so perfect and clear that it might have been taken yesterday.

The change in Edgar's picture left me speechless for a moment. I was still trying to figure it out when I saw Martin hand another present to Constance. It was a book, naturally. I could see that from the shape of the package, even though it looked like Christine had wrapped it.

"I bet I know what it is!" Alice said.

"Alice!" Sophie and Christine scolded at the same time. That's what happens, I guess, when you have *two* mothers standing next to you.

"Give her a chance to unwrap it," Henry's dad said.

"It's a history of the neighborhood," Martin said. "You probably could have written it yourself, but I thought you might enjoy some of the pictures."

"It's lovely," Constance said. "Oh, and you've included a bookmark too."

"A bookmark?" Martin asked, puzzled.

As Constance pulled at the edge of it, my eyes grew wide. There it was again: the card.

A FRIEND WILL CALL FROM FAR AWAY.

I reached into my pocket and found it empty. No card. No marble.

"Hey," Zack said to me. "That looks just like the card we found on the stairs."

"Mr. Corrigan," I said, "is this a practical joke? Because if it is, it's not funny."

"Barbara Anne," my mother said. "I think you and I should go to the kitchen and get the cake."

When we got there, I said, "I know what you're thinking, Mom, but I didn't swipe that card. I don't know how it got in the book."

This, of course, was not true. I was pretty sure I *did* know who had gotten the card from my pocket and into the book, even if I didn't know how. I already regretted what I had said to Uncle Marty. I realized, of course, that Edgar was up to his usual games.

"Now is not the time or place for this conversation," Mom said. "Help me carry the cake."

We lifted it gently and moved back into the other room.

Henry was standing near the window in the dining room, staring out at the rain.

"Here comes the cake!" Sophie said.

"Wow!" Zack said.

It really was impressive. It was the most immense cake I'd ever seen. And we stood there in the darkness, our faces lit by glowing candles, and began to sing. It was the strangest thing—to see each face hovering in the candlelight. For a minute, it felt like we were all . . . ghosts.

"Make a wish!" Alice yelled. "Blow out the candles!"

But before Constance had a chance, a gust of wind swirled through the room and blew out all the candles, not just the ones on the cake.

"What happened?" Renee asked.

Rachel began to wail, and everyone started to talk at once. Henry was the only quiet one. He was still near the window, and in the pitch-dark I made my way over to him.

"Henry," I said. "I think—"

"Shhh," he said. "Just listen."

Then, in the pause, I heard it. An ordinary sound, easy to miss with all that was going on, but familiar to Henry and me, because we had visited before. The sound of the front door closing.

I ran to the hall, and Henry followed me, pushed past me, moved toward the door. "Where are you going?" I asked him.

"Edgar's out there," Henry said.

"It doesn't matter," I said. "He'd never hurt you."

"I need to make sure he leaves," Henry said.

"You can't go out there alone," I said.

By then, Zack and Renee were at the end of the hallway, watching. "Let him go," Zack said.

"Here," Renee said. She handed him a raincoat.

"I don't think this is such a good idea," I said.

"He'll be okay," Renee said. "He just needs to say good-bye to Edgar."

When Henry got back, the three of us were in the hallway, waiting with a towel. Soon the storm began to pass and the electricity came back on. Zack played the guitar, and we all laughed and ate more cake. We finished celebrating Constance's birthday and Henry's return to our lives.

Henry never saw Edgar again. And that night, it snowed for the second time. When I went to Henry's house the next morning to go sledding with him, there they were: the two sets of footprints leading away from her door. And so, I was not surprised by Henry's news. Our friend Constance Leary had died in her sleep.

CHAPTER TWENTY-FOUR

A NEW YEAR

Once Edgar was gone, things got back to normal. We moved through December—from the sorrow of Constance leaving us to the joy of the holidays. Of course, there were still times when we felt scared or sad. After all, the world is a pretty haunted place, and Henry Davis isn't the only one who ever saw a ghost.

But, mostly, we were happy. And on New Year's Eve, my parents let me have a party—with sparklers and Silly String and everything. Zack and Renee got there first, and we were outside in my yard testing out the sparklers when I heard the doorbell ring. Henry. Late as usual.

"Barbara Anne," my father called from the back door, "your final guest has arrived."

"Send him out," I yelled.

"He'd like to see you," my father said. "Privately."

Renee and Zack exchanged a look. "Do not start," I warned them.

When I got to the living room, I saw that Henry had a sack slung over his shoulder. I could tell from the way he was carrying it that it was heavy. "Henry," I said. "Christmas is over. Chanukah is over—"

"Come on," Henry said. "I know you want to know what is inside this sack."

"Okay," I said, trying to sound bored. Who was I kidding? I was dying to see.

"Not so fast," Henry said. "This is a tool that requires some patience and respect. You will have to *learn* how to use it."

"Just give it to me," I said. So Henry opened the sack and lifted out my gift.

"A fire extinguisher?" I said, starting to laugh.

"Portable and small," he said. "We should take a minute to read the directions."

It was red, with an interesting gauge and lever at the top. On the side it said:

1. HOLD UPRIGHT AND THEN PULL
   RING
2. STAND BACK 8 FEET AND AIM AT
   BASE OF FIRE

3. SQUEEZE LEVER AND SWEEP FROM
   SIDE TO SIDE
4. USE CAUTION. IF FIRE CANNOT BE
   EXTINGUISHED, CALL 911
5. THIS MEANS YOU, BARBARA ANNE
   KLEIN

That last one was written on a piece of tape that Henry had attached himself.

"Like it?" Henry asked.

"I love it," I said.

"Are you guys ever coming out?" Zack asked from the back door.

"We're freezing," Renee said. "And we want to light the sparklers."

"And I want to know who gets to do it," Zack said.

"Henry," I answered.

So the four of us went out into the cold December air to shiver and light sparklers and make wishes for the new year.

"Do you know what you're doing?" Zack kept asking Henry as he lit each one and handed them to us. "Why does *he* get to be in charge?"

It was a fair question. After all, it was my house. But I was trying *not* to tell everyone what to do. I guess that was my first resolution.

"Well, it's better than letting Barbara Anne do it!" Renee said. "I'm afraid she might set our shoes on fire."

"Oh, no," Henry said, smiling at me. "Barbara Anne is prepared for any emergency now. You never have to worry."

It's funny the things that scare you. Little things like spiders and bigger things like ghosts. Once Zack was afraid he would be kicked out of our school. Once Renee was scared of being without her mom. Henry feared Edgar. And I . . . well, I guess what frightened me most was not having a real friend. But that all ended—the day I met Henry Davis.

ACKNOWLEDGMENTS

I am grateful to my agent, Miriam Altshuler, and to my editor, Michelle Frey, who guided me so skillfully and waited so patiently for Barbara Anne to arrive and tell her story. Many thanks are also due to the team at Knopf, including Katrina Damkoehler, Ken Crossland, Artie Bennett, Lisa Leventer, and Marisa DiNovis.

A big thank-you to the kids at Green Lake School Age Care Program, whose daily requests for stories are my biggest inspiration.

Finally, I want to thank my family for their collective courage, dark humor, and steadfast love and support during the past year.